DOUBLE SHIFT

DOUBLE SHIFT

DAVID SKUY

Scholastic Canada Ltd.
Toronto New York London Auckland Sydney
Mexico City New Delhi Hong Kong Buenos Aires

Scholastic Canada Ltd.

604 King Street West, Toronto, Ontario M5V 1E1, Canada

Scholastic Inc.

557 Broadway, New York, NY 10012, USA

Scholastic Australia Pty Limited

PO Box 579, Gosford, NSW 2250, Australia

Scholastic New Zealand Limited

Private Bag 94407, Botany, Manukau 2163, New Zealand

Scholastic Children's Books

Euston House, 24 Eversholt Street, London NW1 1DB, UK

www.scholastic.ca

Library and Archives Canada Cataloguing in Publication

Skuy, David, 1963-

Double shift / by David Skuy.

(Game time)

ISBN 978-1-4431-1941-2

I. Title. II. Series: Skuy, David, 1963- . Game time.

PS8637.K72D69 2012   jC813'.6   C2012-901661-6

6 5 4 3 2 1   Printed in Canada 116   12 13 14 15 16

To some old-time heroes who made childhood fun:
Bobby, Borje, Roger, Dave, Ken, Phil, and Tony D.

TABLE OF CONTENTS

1

ANGER MANAGEMENT

The muffins were impossible to resist. Charlie reached out —

"Not before a game," his mom said, slapping his hand.

"But I'm starved. It's either this or I chew off my arm." He took a few pretend bites.

"I just gave you a sandwich," she said.

"That was hours ago."

"Actually, it was forty-five minutes."

She had a point, but he wasn't going to give up. "I think the sandwich was a bit thin, Mom. Coach Hilton specifically said he wanted us stoked for the Wildcats game, and a growing boy can't be stoked when he's starving to death."

She threw her hands up in the air. "I give up. Let me run to the bank first before it closes and then I'll fix you something."

Charlie looked at the clock. "It's getting kind of late. Coach wants us at the game an hour early, and I . . ."

"I can't go to the game with all this money on me. Let's do this: Can you close up? I need you to sweep behind the counter, and put these muffins in the fridge, and stack the rest of the chairs on the tables — and lock the door and set the alarm when you leave. Here are the keys."

"Yeah, yeah. I know the procedure." He had closed the café a bunch of times.

His mom leaned over and gave him a kiss. "I know you do," she said. "I'll take the van and double back and pick you up. Listen for the horn. In the meantime, get yourself something in the kitchen — without making a mess, please. And try to keep it healthy. I don't think you can get stoked on muffins."

"You're wrong, Mom, but I'll do it for you."

"I'm sure William and the Rebels will appreciate your sacrifice."

William Hilton coached Charlie's major bantam rep team, the Rebels. They were defending league champs, and with some newly added talent, the team looked good to repeat. Injuries were a huge problem, however. Four players, all good friends of his, had been badly hurt in a bus accident — not to mention he had nearly drowned! Charlie worried whether the new guys on the team could carry the load until they got back.

"No worries. I'll meet you at the corner so you don't have to make the turn," he said.

"Thanks. I'll see you in about ten minutes." She gave him another kiss and left the café, but not before spinning the sign in the door from *Open* to *Closed*.

Charlie decided to focus on the most important task: food. He really was hungry. Sure, he had promised his mom not to eat a muffin, but would she ever find out? They were sitting there on the tray, helpless, waiting to be eaten. His mouth began to water.

He heaved a sigh and covered them in plastic wrap. She was right. So what else? Charlie went into the kitchen. Bread was always a good start. He took a loaf from the shelf. He could go in the meat direction, but that might sit in his stomach, and they were playing soon. He opened the fridge and a brick of cheddar caught his eye.

"Joyce. Don't be stupid. Rule One. Make the simple play. Go grilled cheese."

He laughed out loud, and wished Pudge, his best friend, had heard that. Hilton had been teaching them a new style of play, inspired by the rule changes in the NHL, a game of constant motion, quick decisions, and aggressive attacking strategies all designed to break an opponent down. It was an intense learning experience, and challenging, and they made lots of mistakes, but every so often it clicked, and then it was hockey magic. To make things easier for them Hilton had created the Five Golden Rules of Hockey. Rule One was Keep it simple.

He turned on the range and added some butter to a pan, and then buttered the bread quickly before sliding in a few slices of cheese. He grabbed a package of napkins from a drawer. Charlie had been bugging his mom lately to let him help cook at the café. He did it all the time at home, but she said he was still too young. At least this once he could feel like a chef. He popped a white cap on his head. After a minute he cut off a piece and took a test bite. He figured it could use more time, so he put it back in the pan.

He heard the shuffling of feet. "Don't tell me you forgot the money," he called out, poking his head through the swinging doors.

"Of course we brought our money. How else could we expect to purchase your mother's delicious treats?"

Charlie's jaw tightened and he steeled his nerve. The four kids he despised most in the world, all players on the Wildcats, the Rebels' archrivals, walked toward him.

"We're simply famished, Chuckles, my good friend," Liam said. "So make yourself useful and serve us."

Charlie locked eyes with Jake, the leader of their crew.

So much had happened since he had come to Terrence Falls with his mom and sister after his dad's accident. But one thing had stayed the same — his feud with Jake.

"Not sure how you missed the big sign in the window. We're closed," Charlie said.

"You don't close until six o'clock. We still got two minutes," Thomas said.

"Don't you have a game tonight?" Charlie said. "You'll be late."

"We'll be late if you don't hurry," Roscoe said. "My dad's waiting for us out front."

"Besides, we ain't worried about the game," Liam said. "We're only playing the Rebels. Total joke of a game."

"Be a good boy and give us a few muffins," Jake said. "Nice lid, by the way. It's a good look for you."

Charlie cringed. He had forgotten about the stupid chef's hat.

Jake nudged Roscoe. "The dude can't deprive us of a snack, can he?"

"That would be wrong," Roscoe said.

"Pure evil," Thomas said.

"You're a bad boy," Liam said, wagging a finger at Charlie.

"He doesn't mean it," Jake said. "Help yourselves, lads." He ripped off the plastic wrap and took a muffin.

Charlie grabbed the end of the tray, Roscoe took hold of the other end, and for a brief moment they were locked in a ridiculous game of tug-of-war.

"Don't mind if I do," Liam said, reaching around Roscoe and grabbing three more.

Roscoe let go. Charlie fell back into a table, knocking two chairs off and spilling the remaining muffins onto the floor. His tormentors roared.

"I was wrong about you, Joyce," Jake sputtered. "You really are funny."

"Do it again. Do it again," Liam chirped.

Charlie grabbed the tray tightly with both hands. "Put those back — now!" he said slowly.

"But we're hungry," Liam whined, waving his muffin in Charlie's face.

Charlie slapped it from his hand

"Look what ye did," Liam said in a fake Scottish accent. "Ye broke me snack. I'm gettin' me another right quick." He picked one off the floor and dusted it off with his hand. "Thirty-second rule," he declared, and took a bite.

Charlie gritted his teeth. Four against one — the helplessness hurt more than Liam's taunts. "I knew you were jerks, but I didn't know you were criminals."

Jake put a hand to his mouth and gasped. "Why, Chuckles, that hurts. It really does. You don't know me at all. All we wanted was a quick snackeroo. We didn't want any trouble, and the last thing I'd want is to hurt your mom's muffins. We love the Rainbow Café. Right, fellas?"

The fellas agreed wholeheartedly.

Jake crumpled a bill and threw it at Charlie. It bounced off his chest and rolled under a chair. "Keep the change, *garçon*."

"I don't want your money," Charlie said.

"Use it to buy some breath mints," Thomas cracked.

"He should buy more of those ladies' panties he likes so much," Liam said.

"Maybe he should get some anti-loser spray," Roscoe said.

"No," Jake said. "What he should do is buy some deodorant for his girlfriend, Julia. Ever smelled that girl?" He plugged his nose and waved his hand in front of his face.

Their laughter echoed off the walls.

"She's not my girlfriend . . ." He regretted the words the second they came out.

"He admits she stinks," Liam roared, doubling over.

"Get out or I'll call the cops," Charlie yelled.

"Ain't we touchy today," Liam said. "Mental note. Don't tell Chuckles that his girlfriend stinks. Gotcha!"

Jake pretended to fire a handgun at Charlie. "See you later . . . and you might want to keep your head up. I wouldn't want to give you another concussion. I really felt bad about that."

"Enjoy your muffins," Charlie said. "They're the last ones you'll ever have from here."

Jake's eyes narrowed. "You're so serious, Chuck."

"Besides, it's not Julia's fault," Liam said.

Roscoe and Thomas were laughing too hard to add a diss.

"You're out of here or I'm calling the cops," Charlie said.

"You said that already," Jake said. "Don't matter much. Not sure I like the Rainbow Café anymore. It's not very friendly."

He turned to leave, followed by Thomas and Roscoe.

"Later, alligator," Jake said as he opened the door.

Liam looked back. "In the second period I'll introduce you to my buddy here," he said, tapping his elbow. "He's very friendly and loves to give kisses." He took another bite of muffin.

Charlie gripped the tray so hard his fingertips hurt. He had told himself a thousand times not to let those idiots get to him, and somehow they always did. Jake had this unbelievable talent of saying just the right thing to get under a person's skin. Charlie could never understand why so many people looked up to him. He was practically the most popular guy in their grade, and he even had a ton of friends in grade 11 and 12.

He quickly scooped up the muffins. What a waste. His mom was going to freak. And when he thought about it, he could have just sold them the muffins and it would have been over. All they had really wanted was something to eat. Now he had made a total fool of himself, ruined the muffins, and given Jake that idea about Julia. One comment on Facebook and it would spread like wildfire.

A car horn blasted. He looked out the window, then

up at the clock. His heart started pounding. He was going to be late — again. Coach Hilton had warned him. The captain was supposed to set the example. But he hadn't even finished closing up. The horn blasted again, this time even louder.

He would have to finish later. He rushed to turn off the lights, punched the numbers into the alarm, locked the front door and raced to the van.

"Sorry, Mom," he said, slamming the door shut. She drove off.

"Was there a problem?"

"No. Nothing. I just got . . . distracted."

"My goodness, Charlie. I waited five minutes for you at the corner. Cars were honking at me like crazy."

He punched his thigh. "I forgot my knapsack. How dumb can I get? I have my homework in it."

"Do you want to turn back?"

He shook his head. "We're late as it is."

"We can swing by after the game," she said. "Okay?"

"Yeah. Sure . . . thanks."

"So who did you say you're playing tonight?"

"The Wildcats — Jake's team."

"Sounds 'epic.'" His mom flicked her eyebrows. When he didn't respond, she peered at him closely. "Isn't that what you kids say?"

"Sorta," he said. "It's just that when you say it sounds a bit . . ."

"Are you suggesting I'm too old to say 'epic'?"

"Not too old . . . just maybe not young enough anymore."

"How about if I added 'Okay, dawg,' or 'Got ya, dude,' or how about 'Awesome, bro'."

"Not really helping, Mom. But I think you're cool."

The light changed. "Thanks. But somehow I doubt that," she said, laughing.

Charlie looked at a street sign. They were still at least twenty minutes away. Hilton was going to kill him. "Do you mind if I listen to the radio?"

"Sure. Just not too loud." She slapped the wheel. "Another red light. We must have bad luck tonight. We might be a few minutes late, Charlie."

It felt like it took forever to get to the rink. He practically jumped out of the van before she had even come to a stop. He ran to the back to get his gear and sticks.

"Charlie," his mom called out.

"What is it?" he snapped. Didn't she realize he was late?

"I forgot to thank you for closing up," she said. "You're a great help, and I don't tell you often enough."

Did she have to say that? If she only knew what a mess he had left: muffins out, crumbs on the floor, half a sandwich on the counter. If he told her she'd probably race back and do it herself, and then he'd never hear the end of it. Best to tell her after the game. "No big deal . . . It was nothing . . . Thanks."

Her window rolled up and she drove to the parking lot. He pushed the door open and shuffled as fast as he could to the dressing room.

Hilton had his Five Golden Rules. Charlie was going to add one: Don't let Jake and his crew get to you. Never again!

2

HOCKEY RULES

The Rebels' dressing room was at the end of the hall. As he got closer he heard Scott and Nick's voices. It brought a smile to his face. Hanging with his buds and joking around in the room was almost as much fun as playing the game. His smile quickly faded when he noticed Hilton and his assistant coach, Jeffrey, off to the side. Hilton did not look happy.

Charlie ducked his head and reached out to open the door.

"Charlie, can I have a word?"

He let the door close and dropped his bag against the wall.

Hilton pursed his lips and glanced at his watch. "I can't imagine why you enjoy being reprimanded for lateness, and I can assure you I find it equally unpleasant. But you really need to make more of an effort. The other boys get here on time, even the ones who are injured."

Charlie lowered his gaze. "I'm sorry, Coach. I was helping at my mom's café and . . ." His shoulders slumped. That wasn't an excuse.

"I'm at a loss as to what to do. We've had this discussion too many times. I'm not going to bench you, but I am starting Brandon's line, and on that first shift please give a thought to how important this is."

Charlie was tempted to tell him the real story but stopped himself. Better to accept responsibility. "I've promised before, but this time I mean it. I know I'm messing up and letting the guys down."

Hilton sighed and a brief smile appeared. "It's also not the end of the world, Charlie. I'm just asking you to focus on this. You're a terrific captain; much of our success is the result of your hard work, on and off the ice. Think of this as another part of your game you need to improve."

Charlie looked his coach in the eye. "I will. It'll never happen again."

Hilton put a hand on his shoulder. "That might too much to hope for. How about we aim at being on time once in a while and go from there?"

Charlie let himself laugh. "That sounds good."

"Great. Now, hustle up. I'll be joining you in ten minutes."

He held up his whiteboard to Jeffrey. It was full of diagrams, with arrows going every which way. Charlie looked forward to hearing what he was planning; learning about hockey from Hilton came in a close third after playing and hanging with his teammates.

"Joyce is in the house," Scott proclaimed as he came in, "which must mean the Zamboni is on."

Charlie dropped his bag next to Pudge. He and Pudge always sat in a corner together, one of their crazy superstitions that had started last playoffs when they won the championship, and it had become a hard-and-fast rule — and there was always a one-in-a-million chance it made a difference!

"To be honest, I didn't expect you so early," Pudge said.

"Mr. Late is done," Charlie said. He unzipped his bag and pulled his pants out. "From now on I'll be opening the dressing room door for you when you get here."

Nick hopped over on his crutches. The big cast was scheduled to come off in a couple of days. "What's this absurd thing I hear about Charlie coming on time?" he said.

"Ridiculous," Scott said.

"The earth would cease to spin on its axis," Nick said.

"The sea would turn to Jell-O," Scott said.

"Oreo cookies would lose their creamy filling," Nick said.

Scott gasped. "Not that. Anything but that. Charlie, please — don't change."

"You guys need to get healthy," Charlie said. "You've got too much time to think."

"Totally untrue. I haven't had a thought since grade three," Scott said.

"And that wasn't really a thought," Nick said. "It was a burp."

"There's a difference?" Scott said. He forced out a burp. "I guess you're right."

"Stop distracting the players," Zachary said. He leaned his cane against the wall. He was also recuperating, from knee surgery.

"But if I do that, what's my purpose in life?" Scott said.

"You don't have one," Nick said. "That's why you should be spending your free time in a cardboard box."

"Let's get dressed, guys," Spencer Wicken said. "We gotta get focused on this game. The Wildcats ain't gonna be fooling around."

Charlie felt himself flush deeply. Spencer shot him an intense look from across the room, and then went back to taping his socks.

Spencer was one of the new players who had joined the Rebels at the start of the season. He was proving to be a formidable D-man, and his defence partner, Philip, was a solid, stay-at-home type like Scott. The Rebels had also acquired a new goalie, Andrew, and now he and Martin represented the best 1–2 goaltending tandem in the league. Three other players, Nazem, Brandon and Will, formed a complete forward line, and their scoring was going to be needed until Zachary and Matt got back.

When the season started, Charlie had been too pre-occupied with the campaign to save his high school to really get to know his new teammates, and now he sensed a rift forming. He suspected that was why Hilton was on him for being late. It obviously bothered Spencer, and maybe the other new Rebels also. At the same time, Spencer could cut him some slack. Sure he was late, but dissing him was not going to make it better.

His buddies all exchanged glances. Charlie shook his head slightly as a sign to let it pass. He reached into his bag and pulled out his shin pads.

Scott wandered over to the door leading to the washroom, a mischievous smile crossing his face, and picked up a cardboard sign. It had become an old friend and constant companion — Hilton's Five Golden Rules of Hockey. Their coach made sure it was displayed before every game and practice.

THE FIVE GOLDEN RULES OF HOCKEY
1. Keep it simple.
2. Forecheck, backcheck, paycheque — outwork the opposition.
3. Never stop moving your feet.
4. The puck travels faster than you — pass.
5. Support your teammates.

"Hey, Nick. I'm thinking that Rule Five is dumb," he said.

Spencer's face darkened.

"I'd go with 'Eat more bacon,'" Scott said.

"I really don't understand why Hilton doesn't let you do more coaching," Nick said.

"It *is* puzzling . . ." Scott said. "Of course, he wants me to focus on rehabbing my shoulder so I can come back and save the team — as usual."

"Team doesn't need to be saved," Spencer said. "The team needs to worry about Rule Two."

Spencer was most definitely not going along with the joke. The dressing room had gone quiet.

"Anyone got some sock tape?" Charlie said. "I'm out."

The twins, Robert and Christopher, a stalwart defence pair, each tossed a roll his way.

"Thanks, dudes," Charlie said. "I'll use one roll for socks, and the other to tape Scott's mouth shut."

"Not a problem." Scott shrugged. "I'm studying to

be a mime." He pretended to be trapped inside a box.

Charlie figured he should keep talking to lighten the mood. "Matt told me he might be able to play in the next couple of weeks. That'll give us a bit more jump up front." Matt had been out with a concussion for over a month.

"It'll throw off the lines, again," Brandon said. "We'll have eight forwards."

Matt was a total energizer on the ice, and he had a sweet touch around the net. Why would Brandon care about the lines compared to that?

"You haven't seen him play much," Charlie said. "We gotta get him back. He'll be our third centre, and create another scoring threat. Then when Zachary, Scott and Nick get back, we'll be ready to roll again."

"One scoring threat ain't enough, I guess," Brandon muttered. He leaned forward and began to retie his skates.

"Yeah — it'll be *awesome* when our best players come back," Spencer added. He also began to retie his skates.

These guys were so sensitive; they always took things the wrong way. But Charlie let it go.

"May I have your attention?" Scott declared dramatically. Charlie prayed he wasn't going to respond to Brandon and Spencer's comments. "Dalton, our beloved manager, has an announcement. Everyone, please, please, please, be quiet and let the poor boy speak."

Charlie relaxed and pulled his socks over his shin pads.

Dalton turned red. "You really do add humour to the dressing room atmosphere," he said.

"Scott's definitely a big joke," Nick said.

"Yes. Well, I do have a brief announcement," Dalton said.

Charlie had recently invited Dalton to be the team manager, and he was perfect for it. He might be a bit fussy over details, and he had a funny way of talking, but he was a good guy and had thrown himself into the job. The team had never been better organized.

"Steve Roberts, who runs our league, has some news he would like to share. Come in, Mr. Roberts." A short man with large, black-rimmed glasses and intense eyes walked into the room. Hilton followed him in.

"Boys, as you know, everyone is concerned about concussions. You can't open a newspaper without a sports reporter writing about it, and look at what's been happening in the NHL. Superstars missing dozens of games; some of them even retiring because of it. Anyway, my mom did some research and some doctors believe a concussion at an early age could be even more serious."

Charlie listened closely. He had suffered a concussion last season, and had a Jake Wilkenson crosscheck to thank for that. He had missed more than a month of hockey.

"We're instituting a new rule from here on in. Absolutely *no* hits to the head will be tolerated. Any head shot gets you an automatic game misconduct. You get two misconducts for head shots and you'll be suspended for five games. Get another, and you're gone for the season. So we're serious about it. Okay?"

The boys nodded. Charlie thought it was a good idea. Hilton held a piece of paper up. "I'll review these rules with everyone. Thanks. It's a good idea in my view. Hockey's a physical game, and that's why we love it. At the same time, there's no place for head shots."

Roberts shook Hilton's hand and waved to the team. "Good luck, Rebels."

"He should have this talk with the Wildcats, not us," Charlie whispered to Pudge.

"I see some suspensions in their futures," he said.

"Let's finish dressing," Hilton said, "and while you do, can you all listen up."

Charlie flushed and began to tie his skates. He was the only one not fully dressed.

"We've struggled recently with some of the new ideas I've introduced, but be prepared to keep struggling. We'll make mistakes, give up goals, and even lose some games. But the important thing is to get better every game, to commit to improvement. Our biggest problem right now is Rule One. We're overcomplicating the game, and that's what I want to talk about." He took the whiteboard from Jeffrey. "Here's the new break-out." He quickly sketched the play.

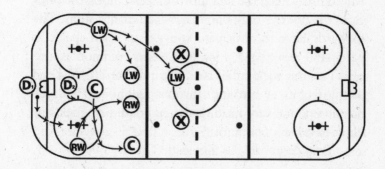

"When there's no pressure on the D behind the net, take it up the side. Centre and right wing cross, and the D can hit either player with the puck. The left winger cuts deep behind the opponent's defence, or goes underneath if a passing lane is not available."

"What if they forecheck us hard?" Spencer said.

"Who can answer that?" Hilton said.

Scott put up his hand. A twitter arose among the guys.

"You need to make a quick decision before the pressure gets you," Scott said. "Pass to the right winger or centre, but if you're in trouble, ice it or lift it in between the two defenceman and the left winger can fight for it."

It was not the wisecrack his teammates expected. Charlie was not surprised, however. Scott was serious about two things: hockey and the not-so-secret love of his life, Rebecca.

"Easy to say when you're in the stands watching," Spencer said.

Scott and he locked eyes for a second.

"You're right," Hilton said. "It looks easy, but I know it's hard. Quick decisions are the key, along with Rule Three: Keep the feet moving. Remember, the puck carrier is not the only one making quick decisions. The forwards have to anticipate and get to open space, at pace. And now that I think of it, Rule Four comes into play. Pass the puck rather than carry it yourself. We need to think of every breakout involving all five players; it's not about one guy making the right pass or stickhandling past five opponents."

"The Zamboni has finished, Coach," Dalton announced.

Charlie reached for his gloves. They were beginning

to look a bit sad. The Rebels' sponsor, Brent, who owned a great hockey store in town, had given them to him last season. Charlie had played a lot of hockey since then. Two fingers had split and were being held together by tape, and the stitching on the side of the other glove was unravelling. He probably needed new ones, but even though his mom never said anything he could tell money was tight. He quickly added a little more tape.

"Give me Brandon's line to start, with Spencer and Philip on D. Andrew is in goal today," Hilton said.

Charlie knew his friends were looking at him. This was not the routine; he usually started. But it was his own fault. He would have to show Hilton that he was worthy of being captain.

"I disagree with one thing, Coach," he said. "We might give up some goals, and we will make mistakes, but we ain't gonna lose any games!"

The boys let out a roar and rose to their feet.

"Re-bels! Re-bels! Re-bels!"

"Rock 'n' roll time, dudes," Zachary said.

"Fast feet — no slowing down," Spencer said.

"Play hard every shift," Brandon said.

"Rule Two, dudes. We win every shift," Charlie said. He slapped his tattered gloves together.

"Re-bels! Re-bels! Re-bels!" they chanted, and followed Andrew out to the ice.

Charlie and Pudge held back. It was part of their pre-game ritual. After everyone had gone, Charlie tapped Pudge's shin pads twice with his stick, and Pudge did the same.

"Gotta win this game," Charlie said.

"Only reason to play," Pudge said.

"Then let's do this," Charlie said.

They punched gloves and together they headed out. Brandon and Spencer could think what they wanted. Until his friends got healthy the Rebels would have trouble winning games, especially against the league's two powerhouses, the Snowbirds and the Wildcats. Charlie jumped through the door and took off the instant his skates hit the ice, carving deeply as he stormed across the blue line and curled down the boards toward the Rebels' net.

3

DROP OF THE PUCK

The puck deflected off the outstretched blocker of the Wildcats goalie. Nazem got to it first and chopped it behind the net to Brandon. Their right defenceman cut off the passing lane in front, so Brandon continued past the net to the corner. The normally ultra-conservative Christopher broke down low from the right point. Brandon hesitated slightly and then passed. From two metres inside the top of the circle, Christopher fired a powerful slapshot on net.

The goalie's left pad shot out. The puck nicked the top edge just enough to send it into the corner. The Wildcats supporters let out a huge cheer. On the bench, Charlie banged the top of the boards. "Talk about luck. He didn't even see it." He sat back down. "We've been all over these guys, and we can't buy another goal."

"We're in their end," Pudge said. "It's all good."

Charlie continued to fret. It was an ironclad law of hockey: if one team dominates and does not score, the other team will. The Rebels had gone up 1–0 early in the first period when Pudge scored off a feed from Charlie; and they continued to pour in on for the rest of the period, but could not add an insurance marker.

A Wildcats defender beat Nazem to the puck and chipped it up the wall to his right winger. Robert did a nice job pinching and the puck rebounded off his leg back to the corner. The Wildcats centre then settled the matter by grabbing hold of the puck and lofting it high over everyone's head to relieve the pressure.

"Charlie's up, with Pudge and Jonathon," Hilton announced.

Christopher collected the puck at the Rebels' blue line while both teams raced to change lines.

"Time for you to stuff in another, Sergeant," Charlie said to Pudge.

"Ready when you are, Major," Pudge said.

Charlie hopped the boards eagerly and swung wide left. Christopher fed him a soft lead pass and headed off to change. Charlie took a couple of steps to cross the red line, and then, figuring his linemates would be near the Wildcats' blue line, ringed the puck around the boards to the far side. Pudge charged across and met the defender head on as he tried to control the bouncing puck. The puck squirted free, and Jonathon got a stick on it and knocked it across the goal line. Charlie was tempted to chase after it. Hilton had been on them recently not to over-commit in the attacking zone and give up a fast break, so instead he hovered a metre above the top of the circle.

That decision proved wise, as the left defenceman came across and hit the Wildcats centre with a good pass. Charlie slid across, laying his stick along the ice to cut off the passing lane. About three metres from the blue line, the puck carrier cut right and banked the puck off the side wall for his right winger, who merely flicked it on into the Rebels' end. Philip made him pay, though, driving him into the boards. The winger responded with a slash to Philip's leg.

The refs kept their whistles in their pockets.

"You gotta call that," Charlie yelled as he scooted past. "How'd you miss the slash?"

"Play hockey, number eight," the ref growled.

Easy for him to say, Charlie thought. He hadn't gotten a two-hander across the leg. Spencer picked up the puck on his forehand and swung toward the slot in front of Andrew. Charlie was first back. He curled at the blue line. The Wildcats left winger was hugging the boards. Pudge was wide left and Jonathon was covering the opposite winger. Charlie noticed the centre getting off and Jake coming over the boards. There was a seam up the middle he could exploit if Spencer got him the puck quickly.

The next instant the puck was on his stick. Grateful for the timely pass, Charlie wasted no time crossing into Wildcats territory. Pudge had a good head of steam going along the left wall, and Jake was coming across to intercept him. Charlie did not want to risk a turnover in the neutral zone, so he hesitated a moment to freeze the left defenceman and allow Pudge to get close to the blue line, and fired it into the corner.

Pudge won the race for the puck and threw it in front. The goalie made a nice play, however, reaching across his body to catch the spinning puck. He pushed off to his left, looking to move it to his other defenceman. Charlie preferred a faceoff in their zone. He put on the afterburners and the goalie was forced to keep it. A defenceman took a threatening step toward Charlie.

Figuring there was no sense in causing a scrum, Charlie veered off to join Pudge in the corner.

"I guess that counts as a shot on goal," Charlie joked.

"I wanted to put it back around the net to you," Pudge said, irritated with himself. "That was a waste of energy."

"We got the faceoff," Charlie said. "And we respected Rule Two — Outwork the opposition."

Pudge pointed to the scoreboard. "It's messed up again."

It read 18–0 for the Rebels. Wishful thinking maybe, but obviously not right. "I don't see a problem," Charlie said. Both refs were at the scorer's box.

"If only life were that easy," Pudge said, tapping Charlie's shin pads with his stick.

Charlie skated to the faceoff dot to the goalie's right. As a left-handed shot, a backhand grip would pull the puck to Philip at the point near the boards. Spencer was in the middle and by far the more dangerous player, and he had a deadly shot. But Charlie did not think he would win a draw against Jake in the Wildcats end using a forehand sweep.

Jake was hunched over at the bottom of the circle, his stick across his knees. Charlie and he had played a few shifts against each other, but not much had happened. Jake, Liam and Roscoe all seemed focused on the game, and that suited Charlie.

Liam stood in the slot. "Easy draw, Jaker. No competition."

That was tame stuff. Charlie ignored him and set up at the dot.

Liam was not done, however. "Hey, pastry boy. Why don't you run along and get me a croissant," he cracked.

Charlie slid his hand down the shaft of his stick. He would win the faceoff to shut Liam up.

"As a friend, I really think you should discuss the art of showering with that young lady we were talking about," Liam said under his breath. "If you don't want the problem to get worse."

Charlie kept his eyes trained on the dot. Just when he thought they were going to play hockey.

"At least tell her to shower after a hockey game," Liam added.

Charlie gripped his stick tighter.

"At least explain soap," Roscoe piped in.

Jake adopted a reverse grip and joined Charlie at the faceoff circle. He leaned his head in so their helmets were almost touching.

"At least tell her to change her underwear once a month," he whispered.

The referee blew his whistle and skated over to them with the puck in his hand.

It wasn't going to stop. Charlie knew them too well. It was going to become a thing — first text messages, then Facebook, and soon it would get back to her. A rush of overwhelming anger swept through him. The puck dropped. Charlie ignored it. Instead he lowered his shoulder and crushed Jake with a check, extending his arms into his chest to finish him off. Jake flew back, knocked clear off his feet, and landed on his back, his helmet banging off the ice. A roar sounded from the stands.

Roscoe dropped his stick. "No way, loser," he yelled, swinging at him.

Charlie ducked away, took a step back, and exploded at the hulking left winger. A solid right hook caught Roscoe on the side of his mask, causing him to drop his hands, and that let Charlie sneak a left hook to his chin. Roscoe's mask slipped halfway up his face. Before Charlie could deliver another blow, two arms wrapped themselves around his chest and twisted him away.

"That's enough of that," a deep voice ordered. The referee dragged him to the back wall. "You ready to calm down?"

Charlie's heart kept pounding away even though he was not winded in the least.

Pudge came over. "You got him, Charlie. Let him brag about that."

Jonathon drifted over too. "What was that about?"

"Back to the bench," the referee barked at them. "You're in the dressing room, number eight," he said, tugging on Charlie's jersey sleeve and leading him to the door.

"I got your number eight for a game misconduct for a blow to the head, and a four-minute penalty for roughing," Charlie heard the other referee tell Hilton.

"What about their guy?" Hilton said. "He threw a punch."

"I kicked him out too," the referee said.

Hilton grunted and turned away. Scott and Nick were in the stands clapping. The Wildcats' supporters drowned them out, however, and Charlie left the ice to the sound of catcalls and jeers. Dalton met him at the dressing room to unlock the door.

"Give me a moment to fit this key . . . yes . . . there we have it." Charlie walked in and flopped down on the bench. "The referee instructed me to tell you that with a game misconduct you are not allowed to join the team on the bench. Fortunately, he did not call a fighting penalty on you, which carries an automatic three-game suspension. At least now we know how the new head shot penalty works . . ." He paused. "That was my attempt to inject a bit of levity."

Charlie stared at him.

"It was a joke."

"Sorry. I'm . . . uh . . . I'm a little . . . Sorry, I didn't hear you."

Dalton rubbed his hands and then clasped them together. "I'm sure this must be quite distressing. While I'm not a player myself, I imagine emotions can get the better of you in the heat of the moment." He cleared his throat. "If you don't mind me asking, what was it that motivated your . . . actions? Some of the guys were wondering."

He could only hope that meant the other guys on the ice had not heard, or at least had not understood, what was being said. If that was the case, he intended to keep it that way.

"It was Jake being Jake," Charlie said wearily. "I lost it. No excuse. Could you tell them, and Hilton, that I'm sorry."

Dalton leaned back into the door. "I will pass your message along, Charlie. I should get back to the bench."

"Go get 'em."

A roar sounded. Dalton poked his head out. "The Wildcats have taken advantage of the power play to even the score. It would appear that number nine has scored."

"Of course Jake would score," Charlie muttered.

"Pardon?" Dalton said.

Charlie gave Dalton a thumbs-up. As the door closed, he slowly untied his skates. The Rebels were down to one centre. He had just levelled Jake and pounded Roscoe — you'd think that would cheer him up. It didn't. He felt guilty. He had let the team down. But how could he allow Jake and Liam get away with talking such trash about Julia?

He took his time, and had only begun to undo the tape on his shin pads when the crowd let out another roar. He shuffled over to the door to look out.

He slammed it shut again. Liam and Roscoe were congratulating Jake on his second goal. It was 2–1, and there was nothing he could do about it. By the time he was dressed and had joined Scott and Nick in the stands, there were two minutes gone in the third, and the score was 4–1.

"Did you have to test out the new rule so quickly?" Scott said.

"It's not his fault," Nick said. "He just forgot this isn't the U.F.C."

"I forgot to use my brain, that's what," Charlie said.

Scott patted Charlie's back. "I do that all the time," he said.

"What went down?" Nick said in a serious tone.

He should have thought something up in the dressing room. "Liam was chirping as usual, and then Jake got into it. I . . . I shouldn't have done it . . . They were just too annoying for words." He pressed a foot against the top of the seat in front of him.

The lady sitting there moved over.

"What did they say?" Scott said.

Charlie gritted his teeth. "It's a long story. They came to the café before the game, and . . . they talked junk about . . . my mom. Can't remember exactly how it started, but . . . I just lost it." He kicked the seat in front of him. The lady turned around.

"Sorry," he said, turning crimson. "My foot slipped."

She frowned and turned back to watch the game.

"I'd do the same if they were chirping about my family," Scott said.

"I'd rather be on the ice right now, to be honest," Charlie said.

"He'll think twice before opening his big mouth again," Scott said.

"Look at that!" Charlie said. He kicked the back of the chair again. "Sorry. I'm sorry," he said to the lady. He got another angry look.

Liam had deflected a shot from the point past Andrew for another goal.

"I don't blame you, Charlie," Nick said. "You can't let them say stuff like that. You had to step up. But maybe the timing wasn't the best."

The rest of the game was a disaster, and pure torture for Charlie. The Wildcats knew the Rebels were undermanned, and they played a dump-and-chase game, grinding the defence down and controlling the puck for long stretches in the Rebels' zone. Halfway through the third the score was 6–2. Charlie, Nick and Scott watched glumly as the goals kept coming. The final tally was 9–2: a blowout.

"We should go cheer up the troops," Scott said. "I think I'll start with a few standard clichés like 'We got that one out of our system,' then move to, 'One game at a time,' and finish up with, 'We didn't play our game.' You got anything, Nicky?"

Nick made a sour face. "How about 'We suck,'" he said.

"How about I do the talking," Scott said, and the three boys headed to the dressing room.

4

ALARM

Hilton was standing in the corridor with Jeffrey.

"Go on in, Scott and Nick," Hilton said. "The boys could use a lift after that. This is one time when I don't want you to be serious."

"Darn it, Coach. I used up my last joke two minutes ago," Scott said.

"Do your best, then. I need to speak to Charlie for a moment."

Scott opened the door. "Gentlemen, on a positive note, you can't play worse than that," he began. The door closed.

"I'm sorry, Coach," Charlie said. "That was plain dumb. I'm gonna apologize to the team. I don't know why I let Jake and Liam get to me. Plain stupid. I cost us the game."

Hilton flicked his pen a few times. "Charlie, I'm not so concerned about the game as I am about you. Forgetful and late I can accept, but unfocused and undisciplined, that's not the Charlie Joyce I know." Charlie crossed his arms and lowered his chin to his chest. "Is there something bothering you that I can help with?" he asked.

He couldn't tell him. "I'm sorry for letting you and the team down," he said.

Hilton nodded toward the dressing room. "Head on in, then."

The boys stopped talking.

"I messed up, guys. I need to apologize — big time," Charlie began. "Jake and Liam said some ignorant stuff and I lost it, and . . . I just blew it. They're not worth listening to, and I cost us the game. It was a stupid thing to do."

After a few moments Scott cleared his throat. "Tell us again how stupid you are."

Charlie let himself laugh a little. "Very, very."

"So . . . more than me."

"That might be pushing it," Nick said.

"Scott and Nick told us what they said," Spencer began. "I guess I understand. But dude, you can't be taking yourself out of a game and leaving us shorthanded like that. Guys diss each other all the time. It's part of the game. You gotta learn to roll with it — or give it back to them by putting the puck in the net."

"Nazem was trash-talking with that number fourteen all game," Brandon said. "Spence is right. You can't take it serious, or else they'll never stop."

"That guy never shuts up," Nazem said. "Not a bad player, though."

Number fourteen was Liam. If they only knew what he was really like. "I get it. Like I said, I lost it," Charlie said.

"We hear ya," Spencer said. "But you can't just lose it anymore. Okay? You gotta think on this. It really did hurt us out there."

"The dude was on about his mom," Zachary said, in Charlie's defence.

"Yeah. I say stuff on the ice too, and I've been dissed way worse," Spencer said.

"I've played the game before," Charlie said. "I get it."

"What's gonna happen next time we play the Wildcats and they diss your mom?" Spencer said.

"Nothing. Because *I'll* be there to put Jake through the boards," Scott said.

"Not if I get to him first," Nick said.

"So you guys will save us again," Brandon said.

"We won't take garbage from the Wildcats, if that's your question," Scott said.

"Great. And we'll have a brawl and we'll lose the game," Brandon said.

"Don't take Rule Five so seriously. We'll handle it," Nick said.

"Thanks for that," Spencer said.

"It's on me, guys," Charlie said. The last thing he wanted was for this to make the tension worse between the old and new Rebels. Besides, they were probably only bummed about the game. "Bad game, that's all. It's over. Out of our system. There are no problems with Rule Five, or any rule. It won't happen again. If it does, you can call me on it. But it won't. Okay?"

Brandon shrugged and muttered, "Okay."

Spencer rolled some sock tape between his palms and fired the ball into the garbage can. "That's good enough for me. But look, we joined this team because it won the championship last year, and now we're in fourth and we've lost three in a row. I didn't sign up for this."

"Don't stay on my account," Scott said.

"Get on the ice already," Spencer shot back.

"Let's be cool, dudes," Zachary said. "Charlie's right. Nothing sucks worse than a loss to the Wildcats. Keep it together. We're a team."

"All teams have a rough patch. We had one last year too," Charlie said. "We'll get over it. We had them tonight for half the game. We put three periods together and it's ours. No problem. We put this behind us and move on."

No one answered. They began to undress quickly. Scott caught Charlie's eye. The usually jovial defence-man looked decidedly unhappy. Charlie made the telephone sign with his thumb and little finger. Scott nodded and he left with Nick and Zachary. Brandon and Spencer were speaking quietly to each other, with Nazem leaning over to listen.

Charlie sat next to Pudge. "Tough one, huh?" Charlie said.

"Losing was the easy part. Listening to Jake and Liam mouthing off was ten times harder."

"I didn't help."

Pudge lowered his voice. "What did Jake actually say?"

Charlie slapped Pudge's thigh pad with his hand. "Ancient history. I can't remember." He laughed as if nothing was bothering him. "You think listening to Jake's bragging is hard. It's way harder watching from the stands. That was brutal. Anyway, hurry up and get dressed. It's weird how much more a dressing room stinks when you're not wearing equipment."

Pudge didn't laugh. He bent at the waist and began to unwrap the tape from his socks.

* * *

Charlie's mom turned the radio off. "Do you boys mind? I have a bit of a headache. It's been a long day."

"Sorry, Mom," Charlie said.

He had only just turned it up. She smiled at him, but her eyes did not have their usual life. She seemed real worn out.

"I have to be up early tomorrow," she said, "so I'll need you to watch Danielle until I get back. You can expect a visit from Hannah too, and, I should warn you the girls are planning an awesome beauty parlour — that's a direct quote from your sister."

"Mom! Last time they tried to give me a manicure."

Pudge burst out laughing.

"I believe chocolate-chip muffins will also be involved, so your efforts won't go unrewarded," she said.

She slowed and turned toward the café. Charlie planned his next move. He had to whip inside and clean up fast enough his mom would not become suspicious — and also remember his knapsack! He had been messing up too much lately. He did not need his mom to find out he had not closed up properly, and she did not need that either!

"Are you okay with this, Pudge?" his mom said. "Do you want me to drop you off first?"

"Don't worry about me," Pudge said. "I'm in no rush. The Rainbow's not far anyway."

She turned again, but a police car with its lights flashing blocked the street. His mom rolled down her window.

"Excuse me, officer. My café is about a block and a half away," she said.

"Sorry, ma'am. You'll have to go around," the policeman said.

Charlie looked farther ahead. There were a bunch of police cars and a fire truck.

"What's going on?" she asked.

"I'm not entirely sure," he said. "There was a little fire. Nothing too serious. Don't know much more. I was just told to close off the street."

"Okay. Thanks. Then things will be fine by tomorrow morning?"

He laughed. "I'm sure they will."

She laughed also. "It's tough to sell bread when your customers can't come to the store."

The policeman looked more closely. "I'm sorry. I didn't recognize you at first. You're Donna, right? I've dropped in a few times at your place. Love the Rainbow Café. Good coffee."

"Thanks. Come by anytime and I'll fix you up a nice latte." She rolled the window up. "Sorry, Charlie. You'll have to get it tomorrow.'

This was a nightmare. His mind raced for a solution. "Pull over here. I'll just run over. Give me the key. I'll be back in a sec. Seriously. I need that knapsack."

"Oh, Charlie."

"Please? I swear — two minutes and I'm back."

She bit her lower lip, and then pulled the car over. "Hurry up."

"You wanna come for a run?" he asked Pudge. He guessed his friend would not want to hang alone with his mom.

Pudge followed him out and they set off at a light jog. "So what's going on?" Pudge said.

"I really did leave my knapsack," he said.

"And . . . ?"

"And . . . maybe I left a mess when I made myself a grilled cheese sandwich — left it on the counter — and forgot the time and Mom pulled up outside the café and I had to run out and . . ."

Pudge held up his hand. "Sorry, dude. I only speak English. I'll make the usual assumption that there's a disaster waiting and you need me to fix things."

"Why else would I bring you along?" Charlie grinned.

The smile slowly disappeared from his face. There was a second fire truck parked behind the first, and although it was dark, he could see a faint trail of smoke rising from a building. He ran a little faster.

A fireman held up his hand. "Hold on, boys. You can watch from here."

"What happened?" Charlie said.

"There was a fire, probably a grease fire. We have it under control."

"Was it the Rainbow Café?" Charlie said.

The fireman turned. "I think that's what the sign says. Yeah. I wasn't first on the scene. The water's been turned off for a while, so I imagine it was more smoke damage than anything."

"Damage! Was anything ruined?" Charlie said. His voice sounded shaky.

"Not sure. Anyway. You have to stay back."

"But that's my mom's café," he said. "I gotta get in there."

The fireman's expression became serious. "Do you have a phone to call your mom? She should come over; the captain will want to speak to her."

"She's waiting for us at the end of the street," Pudge said. "We can run back and get her."

"That might be a good idea," the fireman said grimly. He walked off.

Firemen were walking in and out of the café. A couple of them were putting a fire hose back in the truck. Across the street and down a bit another two firemen were huddled around a fire hydrant.

Pudge pulled on Charlie's sleeve. His face was pale. "We should get your mom."

Charlie remained rooted where he stood. His brain was in a fog, as if he could not quite understand what was happening. He looked around at the trucks and the firemen and the smoke. What if the entire place had been destroyed? What if everything had burned down? Only the fireman said it was just smoke — that was a good thing, wasn't it? But that guy had not actually fought the fire, had he? He was doing crowd control. And what kind of damage can smoke do . . . ?"

"Charlie. Come on. Let's run back. Your mom will be worried and like he said she should speak to the captain." Pudge was pulling on his sleeve again.

Charlie nodded. He took one last look around. The firemen were mostly just standing and talking. Everyone was calm. It didn't look much like an emergency. A few firemen even had their helmets off. As he turned he saw his mom. She was about twenty-five metres away. He walked over to her.

"It's the café —" he began.

"I know," she whispered. A tear rolled down her cheek. She held out her arms and they hugged.

"It'll be okay," she said. "Don't worry."

5

A NEGATIVE DEVELOPMENT

The man placed the coffee mug on the kitchen counter. "This is really, really good coffee."

"Thanks, Fire Marshal," his mom said.

"Actually, I'm a fire investigator. The Fire Marshal's office tends to only get involved with the larger fires. But please, call me Roberto . . . I have to get one of those espresso machines in my house. Really delicious. Thanks."

"It's a commercial-grade machine — it's made for a café, not really a house, so . . ." his mom's voice trailed off.

The investigator winked and pointed his finger at her. "Gotcha. I ain't getting this quality coffee for cheap, is what you're saying."

"Would you like another?" she said.

"No thanks. I appreciate the offer. But I've had enough. My wife has been on me for drinking too much coffee on the job. Keeps me up at night. So it's two cups before lunch, and then I'm cut off. I'm already at my limit cause Frankie and I grabbed one on the way over."

Frankie took a sip from her coffee mug. "You really do drink too much coffee," she said with a laugh.

Charlie squirmed in his seat. He had been sitting in the kitchen listening to his mom and the two fire investigators talking for ten minutes, mostly about nothing. He was dying to hear what they had to say about the café. The fire captain had spoken to his mom last night, but told them they might as well go home because the fire was out and it was still too smoky and wet to go in.

Roberto smacked his lips. "Delicious. Really. So, if you don't mind, Frankie and I need to ask a few questions. This isn't an interrogation. We're not the police. Our job is to try and find out how the fire started. I had a good look around this morning, and I spoke to the captain at the scene."

"We spoke to him too," Charlie said.

"Let Roberto speak," his mom said.

"It's okay," he said. "There's no pressure, and feel free to ask me anything you want. I know this is a difficult time. It's tough when a family business is damaged by fire. Very difficult. We're here to help." He picked up his coffee cup and looked into it.

"Are you sure you don't want another?" his mom asked.

He sighed. "Maybe just one. Thanks. But that's it. Please don't give me another, even if I beg."

"I won't," his mom said quietly, and she got up.

"So anyway," Roberto continued pleasantly, "have you any idea how it could have started?"

Frankie took out her notebook.

"Not at all. I've been wracking my brain thinking about it," Charlie's mom said.

"When was the last time you were in the café?"

"Around six o'clock. Charlie had a hockey game,

and I ran to the bank to make a deposit and then picked him up."

"Right. Great. So when you came back to get Charlie, did you go in?"

"No. Charlie met me outside. We were in a hurry."

Frankie began to write in her notebook.

"Of course. Hockey," Roberto said. "Love the game myself. I have two boys that played. Not bad either; way better than their old man." He laughed at that. "My goodness, I must've driven a million kilometres with those boys. They're grown up now; funny how I miss it."

His mom turned on the espresso machine.

"I got off track there," he continued. "Am I to understand that Charlie was the last one in the store — or the café, rather?" He looked over at him.

"I guess," Charlie said.

"What were you doing in the café before you met your mom?"

"I was closing up. A few guys came in to buy something . . ."

"You didn't tell me that," his mom said.

"Yeah. Well, I didn't think it mattered. A few guys . . . Jake and his friends actually . . . they bought some muffins. Took them from the tray. Then you honked and I came out. Sorry, Mom, but I might have forgotten to put some stuff away."

"Doesn't really matter now, honey," she said. She turned the milk foamer on.

Roberto raised his voice to be heard over the noise. "Did you smell any gas before you left?"

"No, sir."

"Any smoke?"

"No."

"Did you go into the kitchen at all, or use the fryer, or the grill, or the bread oven, or the range?"

His mom gave Roberto his coffee. "He wouldn't use the range," she said. "He's not allowed to."

"Thanks for this," Roberto said. He held the coffee up in admiration. "The perfect latte. Look at that foam. It's almost too pretty to drink, isn't it?" He took a sip. "Maybe not." He put the cup down. "Did you use any equipment, young man?"

A chill ran down Charlie's spine. His mom would be angry. But maybe Roberto knew somehow. Could he? His mind raced.

"Charlie. Did you?" Roberto asked again.

"Yes. The range, for a second. I made a grilled cheese sandwich."

His mom gasped ever so slightly. "When I said you could get something to eat, I didn't —"

Roberto held his hand up. "If I could follow up on that. When you made the sandwich — what was it again?"

"Grilled cheese," Frankie said.

"I love a good grilled cheese sandwich, I gotta admit," Roberto said.

"Me too," Frankie said. "Let's get one after this."

Roberto gave her a thumbs-up. "Charlie, take me through how you made the grilled cheese."

The three adults were watching him closely. Suddenly, Roberto and Frankie made him very nervous. "Like I said. It was quick. Some bread, I buttered it, added some cheese, put it in a frying pan and grilled it."

"Why didn't you use the grill?" Roberto asked.

It had not occurred to him. "Don't know, really. I might not have wanted to get it dirty."

"That makes sense," Roberto said. "Easier to fry 'er up in the pan. You turned on the gas and made yourself a sandwich. Right?"

"Yeah. I guess."

"Do you have any idea why the range was on when the firemen got there?" Roberto said.

"Charlie?" his mom said.

He felt as if he had been punched in the chest. "No — not really. I think I turned it off." He thought about it. Jake and his crew came in. He put the grilled cheese down and went out to deal with them. Then his mom came, and he was so angry he just left. Maybe he forgot? "I can't really remember, to be honest."

"On the counter I found a ball of melted plastic and what looked like charred paper of some sort. Did you perhaps use some napkins?"

Frankie's pen was poised over her notebook.

"I did. I took a package down from the shelf."

"Did you fry the grilled cheese in butter, or something else?"

"I used butter."

"You didn't use oil?"

"No. I thought about it, but decided the butter would be better."

"So there was oil near the range?"

He closed his eyes trying to picture it. There was some olive oil, at least he thought there was. "Yeah. I think so. Olive oil, in a can, against the wall on the counter."

"Right. Thanks, Charlie. We'll discuss this back at headquarters, but it looks like we have a solid explanation. The pan would have heated up, the sandwich would have burned, a small spark, a splatter of butter, and those napkins would catch — and then you have a fire. You were lucky the entire place didn't burn down, really. I think the olive oil caused some discolouration on the tiles and some other surfaces, and the range was affected. But other than the smoke damage and the water, it's not too bad."

"We haven't had a chance to see it," his mom said.

Frankie put her notebook away.

"I really do appreciate that coffee. Thanks. We'll be in touch. I have bit more work to do at the site, and I need to figure out why the fire suppression system over the range didn't kick in. I should have my report to the insurance company in a day or so, and my job will be done," Roberto said.

"Is there going to be a problem?" his mom asked. Her voice trembled.

"We don't deal with that side of things," he said. "We're only investigators. But it truly was a pleasure meeting you both."

They got up and his mom showed them to the door. Danielle and her best friend Hannah came running in.

"What did the cops want?" Danielle asked.

"They're fire investigators, not cops," Charlie said. "They were trying to figure out how the fire started."

"What does it matter?" Danielle said. "It happened."

Charlie shrugged. "They work for the fire marshal's office. It's their job, I guess."

Her question got him thinking, though. Did it matter? What was done was done. More important to fix the Rainbow than worry about a grilled cheese sandwich.

"So how did the fire start?" Hannah asked.

Secrets and Danielle were a bad combination, and the last thing he wanted was for this to get around. "Like I said, they're investigating. I think they're going to do a report. We'll know later, or maybe never. Depends on what they find out."

Danielle seemed bothered. "I don't get why it's such a big mystery. A fire starts in the kitchen; that means the range caused it somehow. Who was the last person to use the range?"

That had taken her about two seconds to figure out. Maybe it would not be so easy to keep this under wraps. Her cleverness irritated him. "How do I know? Let's wait for the investigators to finish."

She wouldn't let up. "But you were there, right? Did you see anyone?"

Their mom came back in. "How about we go over to the Rainbow and check things out?" she said.

"Can we come?" Danielle said.

"Sure. Could you guys tidy up downstairs a touch first, though."

"No problem," Hannah said.

The girls ran off.

Charlie had trouble looking his mom in the eyes.

"Charlie . . . honey . . ."

"I know, Mom. I'm sorry. I might have left the range on. I honestly can't remember. I guess I did — obviously I did. I'm so sorry. Jake and his friends came. I should've told you. And I thought they were gonna

steal the muffins, and I overreacted. I was so mad . . .
I . . . I heard the horn and ran out. That's why I wanted
to go back so bad. I was going to clean up."

"I should have been suspicious when you said you
were going to do homework," his mom said. She was
smiling.

Charlie felt a rush of tears. She was being so nice.
"I'll make it up to you, Mom. I swear. I'll clean that
place so good you'd swear it was brand new."

She reached out and ran her fingers through his
hair, and then gave him a hug. "It's okay. I might have
to pay more for insurance, but we'll fix it up."

The doorbell rang again. Charlie could see a dark
shadow in the window. He knew that shape anywhere.

"Pudge is here. We have a practice later and . . ."

"You were going to do . . . homework?" she said.

Charlie grinned. "Something like that."

He heard the sound of scampering feet, and Danielle and Hannah raced to the door. "It's Pudge," Danielle announced.

"We're on our way to the Rainbow," Charlie said.
"You wanna come?"

"Sure. We got time before practice." He turned to
Charlie's mom. "I'm sorry about the café," he said.
"My dad's really upset too. He told me to ask if you
would like to work out of his kitchen for a while. No
problem, he said."

"That's incredibly generous," she said. "I'll . . . I
should give him a call."

"He should be at the restaurant by lunch. Not sure
where he is now. You could call him there."

"I will. Thanks, Pudge."

Charlie closed the front door after everyone had left and pulled it shut tightly. The handle was cold and it stung his hand a bit. That reminded him — he and Pudge had planned to go to the Hockey Repair Shop to look at hockey gloves. Money had been tight even before the fire. There probably would not be much chance of new gloves now — not that he deserved it.

He held out his hands. "Sorry guys. Not this season," he said to them.

6

AFTERMATH

His mom hesitated, and a grim expression came over her face as she pushed the door open. Charlie followed her in. An acrid smell of smoke struck him. His eyes burned and he coughed a few times. Pudge and the girls coughed too. Without commenting on what she saw, his mom walked past the tables and chairs, through the double doors and into the kitchen. Besides the physical discomfort, all Charlie really felt was relief. It did not seem too bad, other than a swirling, winding streak of black soot that marked the ceiling and a small pool of water gathered near the kitchen.

"This shouldn't take too long to clean," he said to Pudge. "We'll need to sponge off the gunk on the ceiling . . ."

Pudge's head swayed from side to side. He seemed uncertain about that.

"Let's check out the kitchen," Charlie said. For the first time since the fire his chest was not so tight and his head was clear. The fire investigator had said things were not that bad, and he was right. A little elbow grease and the place would be as good as new.

He pushed the doors open. His mom was leaning

against a counter, her eyes closed. A bitter taste rose up in his mouth. Unlike the pale streaks on the ceiling in the main room, the marks on the kitchen ceiling were jet black, and the walls were scorched in a radial pattern starting from the range and fanning out like a peacock's tail feathers. A few packages of flour had burst and the flour had fallen onto the floor leaving clumps scattered about. Mixed into the water on the floor were bits of tattered and burned ceiling tile. Sections of drywall had burned, and other parts looked melted. He could see some of the fluffy pink insulation peeking out from behind the drywall, and some of it was melted also. As the fire investigator had said, a few of the floor tiles looked damaged, although it was hard to tell how much with the pools of dirty water about. The dials on the range were completely melted. It was an utter mess.

Charlie felt so incredibly bad for his mom, and so unbelievably guilty, that he could not even speak. But he knew he needed to say something, to show her how he felt. She had not moved the entire time.

"Mom, it'll be . . . we'll fix this."

"I'm really sorry, Mrs. Joyce," Pudge said. "It probably looks worse than it is. A bit of water damage, for sure, and obviously there's some fire damage. But it might not take too long to fix."

His words seemed to awaken her. "I suspect the insurance company will have a few things to say about that."

"You have fire insurance, right?" Charlie said.

"Of course, Charlie," she said sternly. She walked to the range. "Why didn't the fire extinguishers go off?

They're supposed to be automatic." She peered up into the hood.

Pudge came over to Charlie. "Looks kind of like a black cave. Incredible what a little smoke can do," he said quietly.

"Not so little from the looks of things," Charlie said.

"How'd it start?" Pudge said.

If only he could turn back time! That tightness in his chest was back. "I might've had a hand in that."

"What do you mean?"

He picked up his knapsack from the floor. It was drenched. The entire back had practically burned away and the plastic tabs holding the straps had melted into tight balls. He threw it back down and pulled Pudge from the kitchen. Out of the girls' earshot he told him what had happened.

"Figures Jake would be involved," Pudge said.

Charlie's shoulder's slumped and he sat down. "I'd love to blame him, and of course they were total jerks."

"That goes without saying."

Pudge was the one guy he could trust — and he had to tell someone. "There's a bit more to it, and it kind of spilled onto the ice."

"I figured."

"They got on me about Julia, which was no biggie, but then they started saying . . . well, that she didn't shower and stuff . . . and smelled. That put me over the edge, and we got into a scrap, and that's why I was so mad and ran out of here when my mom honked. I wasn't thinking straight. All I could imagine was them posting stuff online and . . ."

"Now I get it," Pudge said darkly. "I heard Roscoe say something about soap. They wouldn't really spread a rumour like that, would they? People know it's not true."

Charlie ran his hands over his face. This was so frustrating he could scream. "I don't know. If I hadn't gotten all crazed on them, they probably would've just left with their stupid muffins. Something about Jake makes me lose my brain — and now . . ."

"I get why you couldn't tell the guys what the fight was about, and I have to be honest with you — all is not good with the Rebels."

"Don't I know it. I want to blame Spencer and Brandon, but at the same time, I get that they think I hurt the team."

His mom came out of the kitchen. "Not much more we can do, and I find this place a bit depressing. I'm supposed to meet with the insurance agent tomorrow afternoon, and then we can figure out how to fix this mess. My goodness, what a disaster. I can't believe it." She shook her head. "Parts of the ceiling outside the kitchen even got ruined. I can't imagine what this will cost."

Charlie followed her gaze. The smoke had left the ceiling a dull colour, as if a fine mist of grey powder had been sprayed to make a monochrome design. It reminded Charlie of the pages of a black-and-white graphic novel.

Danielle and Hannah came over. "I'm hungry," Danielle said. "Can we get a croissant or something?"

"Not here," his mom said. She looked out the window. "I'll make you and Hannah something at home. It's close to lunch, anyway."

"Aw. Let's go out," Danielle said. "I think my throat needs a hot chocolate from this smoky smell."

"I have hot chocolate at home," his mom said.

"But I like it better with whipped cream and only a café has that," Danielle persisted.

"Danielle! Please."

Charlie could see his mom was stressed. He guessed she didn't want to take everyone out to eat. "Let's go home, Danny. I have some cool stuff I want to show you."

"Awesome. What do you have?" Danielle said.

"You have to wait and see."

"What is it? Come on," the girls chorused.

"No. We have to go. Move it, ladies."

His mom gave him a grateful look. All the way home the girls pestered him about his big surprise, and they raced into the house as soon as his mom pulled into the driveway.

"So what's this super-duper cool stuff?" Pudge asked.

"I've been wondering the same thing myself," Charlie said with a grin. "I think the only choice I have in this situation is to attack with pillows. It's a danger-ous mission, and the risk of death is high. I could use some help. Are you in, Sergeant?"

Pudge saluted. "You can't live forever, Major."

Charlie did not feel like a pillow fight after their visit But his mom needed time to deal with the Rainbow, and keeping things fun and light right now would help.

"Once we satisfy Danielle and Hannah's need for adventure, we should put some thought into the Reb-els. It seems like so much has happened over the last couple months, I've barely had a chance to focus on hockey; and I'm supposed to be the captain."

"You are the captain, and no one thinks you're not," Pudge said.

They went in the house.

"Some of the new Rebels might not vote for me, not after the Wildcats game. It's Operation New Rebels from here on in. They don't feel like they're part of the core group, and we need to change that."

"Come on, Charlie. We're waiting in your room!" Danielle yelled.

"First it's Operation Crazy Girls," Pudge said.

"If we can pull this off, we can do anything," Charlie said. He ran up the stairs. "Prepare to be amazed," he announced.

7

NEW BEGINNINGS

Charlie held the dressing-room door open for Pudge and hesitated for a moment before going in. He chided himself for being so ridiculous; he told himself twenty times that it was no big deal; and yet he was a bundle of nerves as he walked into the dressing room for practice. Pudge and he had talked about the Rebels' problems, and both agreed that it all boiled down to Rule Five. They had to play together, as a team. Right now they weren't.

"How's it going, boys?" Charlie said loudly. He parked himself next to Pudge and unzipped his bag. He figured the best strategy was to make a joke about the Wildcats fiasco.

"I got a text from Jake Wilkenson. He promised to be nicer and to stop spearing and hitting guys from behind. He says that from now on the Wildcats are gonna be a skill team — no more rough stuff."

If crickets began chirping it would not have been more awkward. Pudge looked like he wanted to jump into a hole. Not the best beginning, but he wasn't giving up that easily. "Okay. I admit. I made that up. Jake didn't text me. The Wildcats are gonna goon it up like they always do. Next time we'll step it up. We have a few more games to learn Hilton's system, and they won't know what hit them."

He could have sworn tumbleweed was blowing down the middle of the room. Where were Scott and Nick when he needed them?

"Look at it this way," he said. "At least I'm on time."

Jonathon and Dylan laughed, and the twins even cracked a smile. No such luck with the others. Then it got worse.

"I think we should speak to the coach about assistant captains," Brandon said.

Charlie raised his eyebrows. Brandon wasn't looking at him, however.

"Matt and Nick aren't playing, and we don't have any assistants on the ice, and when Charlie got kicked out, we had no one to speak to the ref . . . or anything," he continued.

"Matt will be back soon," Charlie said.

"Whatever," Brandon said. "We can deal with it when he is. I think Spencer should be an assistant captain for now, and probably should be one anyway."

"Not sure the Rebels' problems are about having assistants on the ice," Charlie said. "We need to work as a team more, out-hustle our opponents, win the battles, and . . ."

"We don't need clichés and stupid rules, if you ask me," Philip said.

"We also don't need to learn a new freakin' style of play in the middle of the year," Nazem said. "I left a good team for this, and it's like chaos."

"It's not chaos," Charlie said. "We'll get going. It's a slump, for sure. When we get everyone back . . ."

"There you go again," Spencer said. "They come back and, like magic, the Rebels can't lose. Philip and me won't even have to show. Scott and Nick can play the whole game."

"We're a team," Charlie said.

Spencer spun a roll of tape around his shin pads and pulled it until it snapped. Brandon and Nazem began to tie their skates.

"That couldn't have gone worse," Charlie whispered to Pudge.

His buddy grunted in agreement and pulled out his skates. "Might have to talk to Hilton," he said.

"Charlie. What's this I heard about a fire at the Rainbow Café?" Dylan asked. "I passed by on my way to band practice, and it had yellow caution tape around it."

Charlie grimaced. That was about the last thing he wanted to talk about. But at least it changed the topic. "There was some damage. No big deal. It'll be fixed soon. A total pain for my mom, though."

Dalton came in. "The ice will be ready in seven minutes. The ladies are almost finished their practice. A friendly reminder from your friendly manager."

"Hi, Mr. Friendly Manager," a few boys joked.

"Yes. Well, hello . . . and thanks . . . Anyway, here's another friendly reminder of our game on Tuesday at 7:45 against the Flames," Dalton said.

Some of the guys cheered.

"Please be there at 6:45 at the latest," Dalton said. "Coach Hilton wants a good warm-up."

"Don't tell us — tell Joyce," Jonathon said.

Charlie forced himself to laugh with the others.

"Charlie, Charlie," Pudge pushed his knee. "The skates work better when they're done up."

Charlie grinned weakly and bent down to tie them up. "They say the mind is the first thing to go," he said.

Spencer stood. "I think I'll be out first to prove my love for the game," he said.

"Sucking up to Hilton is more like it," Brandon said.

"Wants to watch the girls is *really* more like it," Will said.

Spencer dropped his helmet on the butt end of his stick. "That's why I'm keeping the hat off. It's good to publicize."

"You'd be smarter to go with a paper bag," Nazem said.

Spencer grinned. "You might be right," he said, and he pushed the door open.

"That dude will have a date by the time the Zamboni's off the ice — guaranteed," Will said, nudging Brandon.

"Don't I know it," Brandon said. "Let's go. He might need help."

A few others got up and left also. Charlie rifled around in his bag for his gloves.

"You going old-school?" Pudge said.

Charlie gave him a questioning look. Pudge tapped his own helmet.

"I've lost it," Charlie said, tossing his gloves off and putting his helmet on.

"While you're at it, you might want to tape your shin pads," Pudge said.

"I don't suppose I could borrow some?" Charlie said ruefully.

Pudge had a roll in his hand. "Way ahead of ya."

Charlie taped his socks and followed Pudge out. The Zamboni had a lap to go.

"The ladies in question are the Eagles," Pudge said.

Spencer, Brandon and Nazem were talking to Julia, Rebecca and Alexandra. Julia had her helmet off, her face flushed and lightly covered in sweat. Rebecca and Alexandra were in street clothes. They had also been badly hurt in the bus accident and were still not able to play. Spencer appeared to be holding court, and all three girls were laughing.

"Let's go say hi," Pudge said. "I wonder when Rebecca and Alexandra can start playing again."

"Go ahead," Charlie said. "I just have to fix my skate." He knelt and untied his laces. He felt weird joining in after what had happened in the dressing room, and the girls might ask about the café, and he didn't feel like talking about that either. He looked over. It was strange seeing Julia joking around with Spencer. She was usually so serious.

Jonathon opened the door to the ice. "Up and at 'em, Rebels," he said, giving them each a back slap as they filed on. "Can we borrow the boys for a moment, Jules?" he called out. Jonathon and Julia had been neighbours since they were kids and they were good friends.

"When I'm finished with them," Julia replied.

"Actually, we don't really need them," Jonathon said. "They're kinda useless."

"Thanks for the vote of confidence, dude," Spencer said, slipping his helmet on. "So the movie's at seven, right? We should go early and grab a smoothie at the Mercury."

"How about six?" Alexandra said.

"Works for me," Spencer said.

"Us too," Nazem and Brandon said.

"Sounds good," Rebecca said.

Charlie had heard enough and he made a beeline to the ice. In three strides he was at top speed, whirling around the boards and behind the net. Of course, it was no big deal. Julia and her friends could go out to a movie with whomever they wanted. Maybe it bugged him a bit that they had never wanted to go to a movie with Charlie and his crew. On the other hand, he didn't remember asking them. But so what? There were way more important things, like turning this team around.

Hilton blew his whistle to start practice. Charlie dragged his right skate behind him and slowed to a stop at centre.

"Bring it in," Hilton said, and the Rebels surrounded him and took a knee. "Don't get down on yourselves if something doesn't work. The Wildcats game was not our best, obviously, and we didn't do a good job of staying disciplined." Charlie kept his gaze on the ice. "I don't want you to think everything was bad. I saw a couple of perfect breakouts with the defencemen pushing and the forwards covering, and you did play them tough for a period and a half. That's the team we want to become: hard on the puck, lightning counterattack, and a punishing defence. We're just not there yet."

He held up his whiteboard and began sketching a drill. "We'll start with this. Breakout Two — and the possibilities are endless."

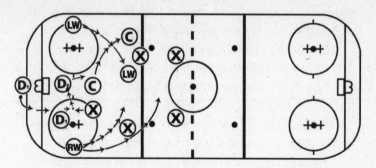

That was greeted with some ooohs and ahhs.

"Again, it's about choice. D1 has the puck. He takes it up the right side and is met with pressure. He drops the puck back to a moving D2. At the same time, the left wing and centre cross and swing wide. D2 can hit either with a pass or keep it himself. The right wing breaks across the top. If there's no pressure, D2 can keep it himself and make a pass once he's past the hash marks, or even past the blue line if he can make it.

"Lots of options, and lots of opportunities to mess up — so let's practise."

They practised for the next ten minutes, and all that time the players seemed to be focused on the messing up part. Twice Brandon cut the wrong way. Christopher seemed overwhelmed by the choices, and invariably he held onto the puck too long and then flung it in desperation, generally for an icing. Charlie almost ran Pudge over, and one time he forgot the play entirely and stood in the slot like a pylon.

When Brandon took over for him, Charlie drifted over to speak to his coach.

"No. No," Hilton barked. "Left wing and centre cross. Winger has to cut wide to give the defenceman an angle. Try it again." He drifted toward centre. Charlie felt awkward, as if he was chasing after him.

"Excuse me, Coach. Can I ask a quick question?"

"Of course. On that last one you need to be the one to gauge where the winger is on the ice. It's not enough to mechanically cut to the boards."

"Right. Yeah. I guess." He didn't want to talk about the breakout. "It's more a question about the team."

"Spencer! Quick. Do it quick. You can't take so much time. Rule Four — the puck moves faster than you."

Hilton tucked a glove under his arm and rubbed his chin with his hand. "I heard about the Rainbow. Your mother must be very upset," he said suddenly.

"We saw the café this morning. There was a bit of damage, some water too. It'll be okay. She has to deal with the insurance company and stuff."

"It must be upsetting for you too."

"It's not that big a deal — a few repairs."

Hilton put his glove on. "Let me know if I can help."

"Thanks."

Hilton blew his whistle. "Will. As I said to Spencer, much faster. Much, much faster. Put some effort into it. You have to get across the ice. For the next few, break it off closer to the blue line. Don't always go for the breakaway. Do it again, Jeffrey."

"About the team?" Charlie said.

Hilton frowned.

"I think some of the guys are having trouble with the new style," Charlie continued. "Me too — I just tried to run Pudge over — but I love it, don't get me wrong. It's hard to unlearn how you always played, and still play instinctively — only that's not it . . ."

Hilton's eyebrows arched. As usual, Charlie felt nervous when speaking to his coach.

"What I'm trying to say — maybe sounding pathetic right now, but . . . What I mean is, some guys are getting a little frustrated and feeling the team is not doing great. I don't know what you can do about it, and I'm all for learning about hockey . . . Maybe we could combine the styles for now?"

Hilton blew his whistle. "Run it again," he ordered. He removed his left glove and tucked it under his arm. "Rule One — keep it simple. This is simple stuff. The problem is you're all trying to complicate it. The solution is not to go back. Think of a mountain. When you're halfway up, you have no idea what's on the other side. You can't see. Then you get to the top, and you can see everything. Hockey's like that sometimes. Soon this will be second nature. Give it a bit of time. Trust me."

"And one last thing . . . um . . . someone mentioned making Spencer an assistant captain, especially since Nick and Matt are hurt," Charlie said.

Hilton gave him a close look. "What do you think?"

Charlie did not really like it. But the new Rebels seemed to want it badly. "I like it. He's a great player, and — how should I put it? — he's vocal in the room. The guys listen to him." He thought it best not to mention which guys.

Hilton blew his whistle again. "Come on in," he yelled. To Charlie he said, "You'll like the next drill: neutral-zone counterattack."

Charlie grinned. "Sounds exciting, Coach."

"We'll get back to that," he said to the Rebels as they grouped around him. "Before the next drill, I want to address something. Charlie has been telling me that some guys are getting down on what we're trying to do here. I respect the feedback, but you have to trust me. For some of the newer guys on the team especially, I understand your frustrations. This might be different from what you expected. It'll begin to click soon. I promise, and it'll make you better players and the Rebels a better team. Okay?"

Most of the guys nodded.

"Also, I've been considering a slight change, what with Matt and Nick still sidelined. I'd like to appoint Spencer assistant captain. Makes sense for when Charlie's not on the ice. Sound good to everyone?"

The Rebels slapped their sticks on the ice.

"Thanks, Coach. I won't let you down," Spencer said.

Hilton sketched the next drill on the whiteboard.

"Assume there's a neutral-zone turnover and our right D gets possession. Immediately, he fires it across to his partner, putting him under pressure because . . . what does he have?"

Charlie and his teammates had responded to the same question countless times the past month. "Choices," they answered on cue.

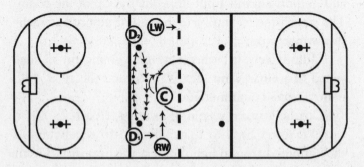

"Correct. Quick pass to the centre cutting up the middle, a short give to the left winger, and he's also got the right winger in the middle. He can even go wide to D1, although D1 needs to be careful not to get caught up ice in case of a deflected pass or some other catastrophic event. Shall we try it, gentlemen?"

Charlie pushed off his knee to get up, and then bounced on his toes a few times. It was time to turn this practice around and energize.

"Let's do this, boys. Full out. It's coming. I feel it," he said.

Spencer drifted over. "Thanks for making us sound like wusses to the coach," Spencer said to him.

"What are you talking about? I . . . I asked about the assistant captain."

"Great. And what's with the new guys not liking the drills? Go Rule Five." He skated off.

Charlie felt the energy leave his body.

"Spencer will start with the puck," Hilton said. "He sends it across to Philip, and that's the signal for the forwards to move. In a game, you'll need to recognize this opportunity. The signal to start is the D-to-D cross-ice pass."

Hilton cradled the puck and then snapped a crisp pass to Spencer. He took it cleanly and rifled it to Philip, who took two steps forward, hesitated, and flipped it up the boards toward Dylan, who waved at it with his stick.

The whistle blew.

"Not bad, but lots of room for improvement," Hilton said. "Charlie was in a better position. Feed it to him. Try again."

The result was no better. Charlie swerved inside the

red line and looked back for the pass. Philip took three strides and tried to hit Jonathon racing across the top from the right boards.

"Think Rule One. You're making it hard on yourself. A three-metre pass to Charlie would solve your problems."

Charlie had his doubts. The problem was more serious, and the situation was anything but simple.

8

DECLINED

Charlie stared glumly at his math textbook. He had a mountain of homework, zero motivation, and he'd just invited his buds to come over and watch the hockey game tonight. He ran his finger down the page to find the next problem. Voices from the hallway interrupted. When it came to math he was always ready to be distracted, and he began to listen.

"Yes, Mrs. Joyce. We thoroughly reviewed the fire investigator's report. I'm not at liberty to provide it to you. Sorry."

"But how can I respond to it if I can't read it?" his mom said.

"I understand how you feel, but this is an internal report. We paid for it, in effect. We also based our decision on it, and the findings are clear. As I told you on the telephone, the decision is final. We're very confident about it. I need you to sign on the line at the bottom corner to indicate you acknowledge receiving this letter."

"I'm not signing anything," she snapped.

"Then I will provide you with this letter indicating you refused to sign the acknowledgement . . ." Charlie did not hear for a moment. "Here's the letter that out-lines our position. Do you have any other questions or concerns?"

"Questions or concerns? Seriously? I have a fire and my insurance company won't pay me. Everything is fantastic."

That did not sound like his mom. She was never sarcastic and rude.

"If you don't have any further questions or con-cerns, then I'll wish you a good day. I hope if we meet again it will be under better circumstances."

"I hope we don't."

"Good day, Mrs. Joyce."

Charlie heard his mom gasp for air and breathe deeply several times. Then he heard a loud bang. It sounded like the front door being slammed. He went into the hall. His mom looked over at him.

"Would you please tell your sister to come up to the kitchen? I need to speak to you both."

He looked around. "Did you hear that noise?"

"I did," she said.

"What was it?"

"Please get your sister."

It did not sound like a request. He went downstairs and found Danielle flopped out on the couch watching TV. "Family meeting, D. Come on up," he said.

"I'm watching."

"I can see that. Mom wants to talk to us."

"Later."

"I think not. Come on."

"Go away, Charlie."

He sighed. "Don't make me drag you up there. You

know I hate all forms of violence."

"Bring it, little man."

He launched his attack from behind the couch, rolling over the back, careful not to land right on her. She grabbed a pillow and got in a direct head shot. Charlie pulled a cushion over her and did a couple of light belly flops.

"I can't even feel that," she squealed in between giggles. "You're pathetic."

"Charlie! Danielle! Upstairs. Now."

It was time to hurry this up. He threw the cushion off, scooped her up and began spinning around as fast as he could. It was his go-to end-the-wrestling-with-Danielle move.

"Okay. Okay. Let me walk. Let me walk."

Laughing, she staggered toward the stairs.

"Not bad, Danny," he encouraged.

She weaved a fair bit, and knocked into a chair, but otherwise made it there unscathed. She held her arms up in the classic muscle-man pose. "I declare myself the Dan-stroyer, crusher of brothers, undefeated and totally awesome."

"Let's call it a draw, then," Charlie said. He pointed upstairs. "Time to boogie, girl. Mom's a bit frantic today."

"How come?" she said.

"Don't know. Something about the insurance on the café. We'll find out soon enough."

"Hey, Mom," Danielle said, as she walked into the kitchen. "I'm hungry."

Their mom sat at the kitchen table, dabbing the corner of her eye with a tissue. This was the second time since the fire he had seen her so upset. It almost made him cry. He took a few deep breaths. Her face was pale and her eyes were puffy. "I'll fix you something in a minute. Can you sit down? We have to discuss a few things. There have been some changes, or at least the insurance company made a decision that will force me to make some changes."

They sat. Apart from the hum of the fridge it was completely quiet. Charlie prepared himself for bad news.

"I just spoke to the insurance adjuster," she continued. "Apparently, the investigators have decided that we were partly to blame for the fire. . ."

The bottom of his stomach began to churn, and a gross taste rose up to his mouth.

". . . along with the company that installed the hood over the range. Every restaurant must have a fire suppression system and . . ." She bunched her right hand into a fist, and then slowly put it back on her lap. "To make a long story short, the system wasn't turned on. Can you believe it?" She laughed, but not in a happy way. "The insurance company is holding me accountable. How was I supposed to know? And to make matters worse, the company that installed the hood is not in business anymore."

"Can't we complain to someone?" Charlie asked.

"I will need to get a lawyer and fight this. It's completely unfair. Sure the range was left on, but the system is there for exactly that type of thing. What kind of incompetent dolt installs a fire system and then doesn't turn it on? I mean, really."

"I started the fire," Charlie said quietly.

His mom leaned forward and put her hand on his. "You don't own this, honey. Sure, you left it on. We all make mistakes. And maybe I have to pay a bit because you're underage and can't legally use the range. But I'm not going to take the blame for a faulty fire system."

Charlie's head was spinning. *He wasn't legally allowed to use the range?*

"I'll handle this," she said. "My main concern is that I owe some money to the bank and to the landlord, and with the café closed I am going to have trouble making my payments. And of course the lawyer is going to cost me . . . well . . . hopefully less than a bundle. Pudge's dad has been a dear and he's going to let me work in his kitchen in the mornings. They don't open until eleven o'clock for lunch, and so I won't be in anyone's way. I've got some baking work for other cafés and restaurants, and if I can build that business I should be able to keep things going until . . . well . . . until the lawyer we get changes the insurance company's mind and they give us the money to fix the café. I have to speak to the bank too. If they'll cut me some slack then . . ."

She clasped her fingers together and pressed them into her lap.

"I'll have to work in the mornings. Very early in the morning, as in four o'clock." His mom turned to him. "I'm going to have to rely on you guys a bit more around here to help out with stuff like breakfast and getting off to school."

"Charlie can't make breakfast. He's useless."

"Thanks, Danny," Charlie said.

"He'll learn," his mom said, smiling for the first time. "I'll also need you guys to help me with cleaning and getting your homework done on time, and probably I'll need Charlie to take Danielle to drama, which won't be too bad since you can walk. Hockey's a bit more of a chore, but you could go by bus." She tried to smile; but to Charlie it only made her seem more upset. "The first time Grandma and Grandpa decide to go to Florida for the winter . . ."

"None of that's a problem, Mom," Charlie said. His heart was pounding. He was going to make this right. "Whatever you need, and you can tell Danielle that actually I'm the best breakfast-maker in the country — the world champion, actually."

"You can't even beat me in a wrestle," she said.

"That's because you cheat," he said.

"No way!"

His mom held up her hand. "Hold on a sec. One more thing." She clenched her hands in her lap again. "A friend of mine, Theresa — you may remember her, Charlie, you met her once years ago when Danny was only a baby — she recently opened a restaurant, and she needs a pastry chef. And there's a good chance she'll let me become a part-owner."

Charlie almost collapsed with relief. She was making it sound like it was the end of the world. Sure, it would be awful if the Rainbow Café did not reopen. But his mom was the best baker in Terrence Falls. Everyone said so.

"I'll miss the Rainbow," Danielle said. "Can Hannah and me still have a snack at this new place?"

"That's a sweet question, cutie," she said. "You've both been so strong, dealing with Daddy's accident, and coming to Terrence Falls and doing so well here.

But . . . unfortunately, my friend's restaurant is not in Terrence Falls."

Danielle looked confused. "Then how can you work there?"

Charlie's heart did a flip, and he found it hard to breathe all of a sudden.

"It's in Stanville, Danny," she said softly.

"What?" Danielle said.

"Which is why —"

"You're kidding!" Charlie said. "We have to move — for real? There must be a restaurant in Terrence Falls. I could ask Pudge's dad . . ."

She held her hand up. "We're not moving yet. Like I said, it's only a maybe. I wanted you to know about it, that's all. For now, I need you both to help me out at home, and focus on your schoolwork so I don't have to worry."

"I could get a job, like Matt did when his dad got laid off," Charlie said. "I can do roofing, work at a restaurant, anything. Then we'd have more money for the bank and the landlord."

"That's my Charlie, always solving problems," his mom said. She rubbed his arm. "But you're so busy with school and hockey, and now with helping at home and taking care of Danielle, you won't have much time for work."

"But me and Hannah are in the school play together, remember?" Danielle said.

"I know, honey."

Danielle started crying. "I don't want to leave. We just got here."

"It's my fault," Charlie said flatly. His head made

him feel as if he were floating on air, but his stomach felt tight and heavy. "I used the range even though I knew I wasn't supposed to, and then I forgot to turn it off."

"I told you, you can't blame yourself," his mom said, almost angrily. "This is on the insurance company. Things happen, sometimes bad things." She closed her eyes for a few painful seconds. "I believe we all know that."

All three sat quietly for a moment.

"You can go watch TV again, dear; and don't worry about Stanville." She raised Danielle's chin with her finger. "Okay?"

"I won't tell Hannah," Danielle said. "She'll cry too much." She hugged her mom. "I'm going to watch TV."

His mom looked at him. He couldn't meet her gaze. Leave Terrence Falls? For real? The Rebels, his friends, school — all gone. He could not let that happen. He would get ten part-time jobs before that. The doorbell interrupted his dire thoughts.

"Perfect timing," his mom said. "Who could that be?"

He had forgotten to tell her about his friends. "Uh . . . I invited some of the guys over to watch hockey. Sorry, I should have told you."

"That's wonderful," she said. "It'll be nice for you — take your mind off this . . ."

Danielle poked her head into the kitchen. She was holding the phone. "Can I invite Hannah for a sleepover?" Danielle said.

"I have to go out later and meet Pudge's father at his restaurant. Maybe another night is better."

"I'll babysit," Charlie said.

"I'm not a baby," Danielle said.

"I meant, I'll watch the two young ladies."

The doorbell rang again. His mom pointed toward the front door. "Your friends?"

"No probs, Mom. I'll feed the girls, even play with them a bit, and get them to bed. I promise."

"Will you agree not to give Charlie a hard time?" she asked Danielle.

"We'll be good as gold — but only this one time."

She gave them each a kiss. "You're both great kids, and I'm very proud of you. Thanks."

Danielle dialled a number. "Hey Hannah, you can come over. My dumb brother will watch us . . ." She drifted away.

"You should get the door," his mom said.

He crossed his arms. "I should tell them to go home. I'm not into it," he said.

She got up and grabbed him by the arms. "It's one more challenge, but we're still together, still a family. We have another bump in the road, that's all."

"We seem to have more bumps than other people," he said. The doorbell rang three times in a row. He left before she responded.

"Hey, Joyce. Trying to freeze us to death?" Scott bellowed, as he marched into the house. "There's a little thing called winter, and he's introducing himself again."

Pudge, Matt and Nick followed him in.

"Mind your manners, little boy," Nick said to Scott, "or you won't get your warm milk tonight." He poked him with his cane.

"But . . . but . . . how will I ever get to sleep?"

Zachary hobbled in. "Yo, dudes. Hall party?"

"Charlie's decided it would be more fun to stand at

the front door and make funny faces all night," Scott said.

"If the hockey game is boring that's a good fall-back," Nick said. "Not your best idea, though, to be honest."

"Not his worst, either," Scott said. "That was inviting you."

"That glass of milk is so gonzo," Nick said.

"We could try watching the game," Charlie said, hoping he sounded normal. "But I really like the hall idea too."

"So let's leave Nick here and go downstairs," Scott said.

Charlie noticed something. "Nick, no cast. That's progress, isn't it?"

He sighed and tapped his knee with a cane. "Barely. Now it's physio, physio, physio. I went this morning. My leg has the strength of spaghetti."

"That's weird. I didn't expect your leg to get stronger in a cast," Scott said.

"Dude, physio is the worst," Zachary said. "My knee kills and the guy keeps bending it and making me work out. Use it or lose it, he keeps telling me. And when I tell him I'm happy to lose it, he orders me to do more anyway."

"At least you guys can work out," Matt said. "With my concussion all I can do is wait."

"When is the waiting over?" Zachary said.

"I'm waiting to find out," Matt said, to the boys' amusement. "Actually," he added, "I've been symptom-free for about two weeks. I go one more and the doctor should clear me to play."

"Please don't tell Spencer or Brandon I said this, and I'm not making a joke here, but I can't wait," Charlie said. "We're barely treading water. Last practice was a disaster. I mentioned to Hilton, in a general way, that some of the guys are unhappy about the new system, and then Hilton tells that to everyone and Spencer thinks I dissed the new guys. The new Rebels regret coming to the team. They don't think much of me as captain; the dressing room is about as much fun as homework and we've got a game in two days."

"What is this strange word he uses — *home-work*?" Scott said very slowly.

"Maybe I should talk to Spencer and Brandon straight out," Charlie said.

"I say forget the talk. You gotta prove it on the ice," Zachary said.

Nick tapped the floor with his cane. "Nothing will be solved without us sitting on our butts and watching the hockey game. We must go downstairs forthwith . . . or fifthwith . . . or sandwich . . . or now."

"Did you say sandwich?" Scott said, licking his lips. He put a hand to his ear. "Hark. Do I hear a life-form in the kitchen?"

"*Shh*. I will investigate," Nick said.

"The boy's an idiot," Scott whispered. "He's going to ask for a sandwich and forget about dessert — and appetizers." He tiptoed after him.

"Hello, Donna," Nick said. "How are we today?"

"I'm quite well, Nick. How's the leg?"

"The head's the real problem," Scott answered for him.

"And how are you, Scott?" she said.

"Fabulous, Donna." He patted his stomach. "It has been a long time since my last meal, however, and I am quite light-headed — starving, really. Not that I'm complaining. It's nice of Charlie to have us over, granted the hallway thing was dumb —"

"Would you boys like me to make you a snack?" she interrupted.

"Not if it's a bother," Scott said.

"I'll see what I can do," she said.

"You're a wonderful person," Scott said.

"Didn't you finish supper fifteen minutes ago?" Nick said.

Scott gasped. "Has it been that long? No wonder I'm dizzy."

"You boys head down. I'll see what I can do about Scott's dizziness."

"To the dungeon," Nick said, in a deep voice.

They trundled to the basement. Danielle's head popped up over the couch.

"Nuh-uh," she said. "Hannah's coming over in five minutes and we're watching a movie."

"You can watch the TV in my bedroom," Charlie said.

She lay back down on the couch. "Nah. It's too small. You can watch there if you want."

"There are six of us," Charlie said.

"Not my problem."

"Danielle," he said sternly. "Don't make me toss you out — in front of everyone — and embarrass you."

"I'm the Dan-stroyer, don't forget. No one tosses me." She flicked the channel.

Charlie felt his temper rise. She could be such a pain!

"Charlie!" his mom called down. "I'm such a scatterbrain. I lost track of time. I've got to go. There are muffins and fruit in the fridge. Help yourselves. See you, boys."

"Bye Donna," the boys chorused.

Charlie took a deep breath. He had promised to take care of his sister and Hannah, even to play with them, and his mom would not be happy to hear he had a big fight with Danielle over the television.

"Guys, I think it would be more fun to watch in my bedroom," he said.

"Six guys huddled on a bed?" Scott said.

"Far away from the air hockey table?" Nick said.

"And comfortable seating?" Zachary said.

"If you can convince Danielle to change her mind, go ahead," Charlie said, and he headed upstairs.

"Run away, cowards!" Danielle jeered, as his friends followed him.

9

ONE STEP FORWARD

The Flames left winger dumped the puck deep into the Rebels' zone and then headed off to change. Charlie put his head down and powered his way back. They would have lots of time because all the Flames forwards were heading off. Pudge was wide left and Dylan was on the right, near the hash marks. Spencer was first to the puck. He hesitated slightly, rounded the net and cut up the ice sharply to Andrew's right. The new breakout! Charlie cut to the boards almost instinctively. Maybe Hilton was right. Maybe they were getting the hang of things. Out of the corner of his eye he saw Philip head to the bench to change up.

He leaned hard on the inside edge of his left skate and curled toward the wall at the top of the circle. Maybe he should have gone a bit deeper into their zone, but he did not have the time. Charlie looked back at Spencer and readied himself for a pass.

It didn't come. Spencer continued up ice, with a forechecker bearing down on him.

"Spencer," Charlie yelled, tapping his stick.

Close to the blue line Spencer tried to feather a pass up the middle, but he had waited too long and Pudge and Dylan were bunched up together in the neutral zone. Dylan came to almost a complete stop to collect the pass.

Thud!

Spencer was flat on his back, courtesy of a good hit from the Flames forward. A defenceman poked the puck off Dylan's stick, and another forward who had jumped onto the ice from the bench swooped in to gobble up the puck. Charlie pivoted on his left skate and turned to face the rush, holding his stick in front of him, with his right hand and his left glove out wide. It was a three-on-two. He assumed Spencer would move over, so he kept to the right side of the ice. To his surprise the puck carrier ignored Charlie completely and headed straight at Spencer, which Charlie found bizarre since he was the forward, and he always went after a forward who was forced to play defence against an odd-man rush.

Thud!

Charlie fell to his knees. It was as if he had backed into a tree. The crowd was screaming, and Charlie looked behind him. Spencer was sprawled on the ice. Three Flames stormed in alone on Andrew. The player with the puck faked a shot and passed across to his teammate camped out at the top of the crease. Andrew dropped into a butterfly. The puck slid back across, and a Flames forward slammed it into the net. Andrew slapped his stick on the ice and looked over at Charlie and Spencer.

Spencer got up without a word and went to the bench. Charlie got to his feet slowly, the wind knocked out of him. Against the boards the Flames players were congratulating the goal scorer — most of them laughing.

Charlie glided to Andrew on one foot.

"Can you tell me what happened there?"

"You backed into Spencer, dude."

"Why was he behind me?"

"He got hit. He just got up."

"In all that time he only just got up?"

"He took a big hit."

Charlie was furious. It was not that big a hit. That was laziness. They had managed to break the first four Golden Rules on one play, and not just any play, giving up a goal with three and a half minutes left in the third to let the Flames go up 2–1. An old idea came to him, something his dad had once said. *The only thing you can control in hockey is effort.* He knew what he had to do. It might not work, but nothing is guaranteed in life. He was going all-in on Rule Five. If it failed, then the Rebels' season was done.

Brandon's line had come over the boards for the draw. Andrew backed up into his net, crouched over with his glove and blocker resting on the top of his pads. Charlie put his arm over the crossbar.

"You aren't giving up another goal, even if it's a five-on-nothing. Okay? It's focus time. Stop the puck with your teeth if you have to. We are tying this game up. Okay?"

Andrew was wide-eyed and did not seem to know what to say. He nodded. Charlie slapped his pads as hard as he could. "We're counting on you. We're Rebels, not a bunch of wusses that fall apart. You're the man. We cannot give up another goal and win. Cool?"

Andrew straightened up and looked Charlie in the eye. "They won't score," he said.

Charlie gave his pads another whack. A referee skated over.

"Change up, number eight, or you'll get a delay of game penalty," he said.

Charlie headed to the bench. Zachary opened the forwards' door. He hopped over the boards at the defencemans' end. He wanted Spencer to hear this. The whistle blew and the referee dropped the puck, but he didn't care.

"I want every guy here to forget about this game so far," he said loudly enough for his teammates to hear. "That's done. Nothing to be proud of either. For the past few weeks it's been all whining and complaining. All excuses and reasons why we weren't winning. Here's a newsflash! We aren't winning because we don't deserve it. We suck right now. We suck because we aren't trying. Too busy feeling sorry for ourselves — and that includes me — and every guy on this bench."

"Hey, dude," Spencer said. "You ain't the coach, and . . ."

Charlie cut him off. He needed to get this out — for the Rebels. "I know I'm not the coach. Our coach has been trying to get us to be a team all year, and we're too busy worrying about ourselves. I've been the worst, going on about the guys that are hurt and how it'll be okay when they get back. Maybe it will. How do I know? And maybe some of you new Rebels are too worried about getting blamed because we're losing instead of worrying about Rule Two. Cause we haven't outworked another team in ages."

He snuck a glance at the scoreboard. "We've got three minutes and eighteen seconds to tie this up. We do it as a team, or we mail the two points in and let's fold the Rebels and stop playing!"

Charlie was so worked up he could hardly breathe. All the guys were looking at him. Hilton was also looking at him, his arms folded firmly across his chest, his face stern and inscrutable.

"Forget the first four rules. We only have one rule to worry about — the last. What do you think, Spencer?"

Charlie took off his glove and held out his fist. Spencer stared out at the ice for a good ten seconds. He stood up, took off his glove, and they bumped fists.

"This game is freakin' ours, Rebels," Spencer roared.

Hilton walked off to the other end of the bench. Charlie followed him to the forwards, giving each player a slap on the back and some words of encouragement. Pudge tapped his shin pads with his stick and nodded when he sat down. But he did not say a word.

The Rebels won the draw and Will got the puck into the Flames' end, but not deep enough. A defenceman was able to knock it off the wall and out. For the next thirty seconds the two teams traded possession, neither able to mount any real pressure. Christopher came to the bench and Spencer flew over the boards. Finally, a Flames forward got the puck at centre and fired it at Andrew. Brandon raced over to change.

The puck had been dumped into the right corner, and Spencer was battling a Flames forward for control. Charlie's primary responsibility in his own end was to make sure the slot was secure. Robert had not shifted yet, and he was already there. Charlie knew he could count on the dependable defender, so he figured he should help Spencer. Good thing too, because the Flames left winger had moved in. Spencer had the puck in his skates. The second forechecker snuck in behind him and poked at it, trying to snake it out of the scrum. Charlie had to do something or eventually he would get it.

"Spence. Kick it down low," Charlie shouted.

Spencer did not hesitate. Charlie stretched out with his right hand and stopped the puck. The Flames centre was right there and laid the body on him.

Crash.

Charlie's face pressed up against the glass. His knees almost buckled. Rule Two, he reminded himself. He reached out desperately with his right skate to trap the puck with his blade. The Flames centre pushed against him again, and Charlie pushed back, shoving his butt into him to give himself some room. Leaning hard on his stick, he was able to dig the puck out from the boards. Unfortunately this player must have heard of Rule Two also, and he had no intention of making things easy. He rammed his knee behind Charlie's leg to knock him off balance, and slipped to his right to cut off the side wall. For a moment the game seemed to stand still, two players straining every muscle and nerve to get clear of the other.

Charlie's legs trembled, his arms were heavy and his chest was tight. The Rebels needed to get the puck out. There was probably less than two minutes to play. Out of the corner of his eye he saw Philip sneak to the far side of the net. Charlie bent his knees and slid his left hand down the shaft of his stick. He spun his hip into the Flames centre again, and with the puck on his back-hand reached around the stubborn forechecker and flicked the puck off the boards behind the net. In one motion Philip fired it around to Pudge, camped out at the hash marks. The left winger stopped the careening pass with his right skate.

Last season Pudge would have banged it off the boards to try to get it out. Not now. He did what Hilton had been preaching for weeks, curling into the middle of the zone near the hash marks, and when the right winger pressured, he calmly passed it to Philip curling back to the wall on the left. With no forechecker to worry about, the Flames right defenceman had to give up the blue line and Philip skated it out. Charlie headed up ice. A quick glance back showed the Flames centre was still in the Rebels' end, as was his right winger. All his teammates had joined the attack, Pudge charging up the middle, Dylan to his right, and Spencer trailing.

Philip headmanned the puck to Pudge, who flung it wide to Dylan. He took a stride and chipped it off the wall to the hard-charging Spencer. Philip slowed at the left point, and Dylan hung back to cover the right, which left Charlie free to keep going — but could he make it in time? Pudge swerved sharply to the right at the top of the circle. Spencer faked a pass and drove deeper along the wall, holding his left arm out to ward off the Flames defenceman. He could not get around him, however. The defender played him tough. Unable to get the angle, Spencer opted to continue around the net. Pudge cut off to the right corner, and Spencer backhanded a pass behind the net to Pudge.

A winger came over from the far side to mark him.

Charlie faked left and made a beeline to the right post, hoping for a quick pass from Pudge, and also that the winger would be passive in defence. That did not happen. A defenceman dropped to one knee to cut off Pudge's passing lane, and the winger hustled back to keep Charlie to the outside. Pudge shook his head to Charlie and passed it back to Spencer, who had remained behind the net.

Charlie spun, his back to the net. The winger cross-checked him on the arm and again in his ribs. He was going to get a chance, whatever it took. The defenceman who had been guarding Pudge kept with him, while his partner pressured Spencer. Charlie guessed the other Flames forwards were covering the point. If he could not find an opening, they would have to try and cycle for an opportunity, and time was running out.

The winger turned sideways and wrapped his stick around Charlie's stomach. Charlie did a spinning 360-degree leap to his left to get away.

"Pass!" Spencer screamed.

Charlie landed about two metres from the goal line — in perfect time to find the puck. Spencer had anticipated his move and lofted it over the defenceman's stick. A one-timer was his only option; but the goalie would know that and he would drop to a butterfly and take away the bottom of the net. Charlie decided to take a chance. He dug his blades in, bending deeply at the knees, and rolled his wrists with all his might. The puck rocketed practically straight up.

Ping!

The puck caught the bottom half of the crossbar and ricocheted at an angle back in front. Spencer slid in from the side and whacked at it. Pudge came in from the other side and tried to bull his way across, but a defender held him off. Charlie felt himself cross-checked from behind in the small of the back. No way he was going down, despite the force of the blow and the pain that travelled up his spine. He leaned on his stick and bent his knees even deeper. The goalie was down and reaching forward with his glove. That meant only one thing. The puck was in front.

Without knowing where the puck actually was Charlie thrust his stick under the goalie's hovering glove. He felt something! He pulled back. Then another cross-check into his back caused him to gasp and stagger forward a half-step — but not before dragging his right skate to keep control of the black disk that had appeared almost by magic on his stick. He took one quick step to his left to free himself from the mass of bodies in front. The top half of the net was open. Charlie snapped his wrists. The goalie threw out his blocker.

"Yeah, baby. Yeah, baby. Yeah, baby. There's some Rule Five for ya!" Spencer screamed. He had his arms around Charlie's neck and he was jumping up and down. Seconds later Pudge was pounding him on the back, and Philip and Dylan joined him. Sure, it was only a regular season game, and they had only tied it up. But it felt like a huge victory to Charlie — and obviously to his teammates too.

"You were like a wild animal charging for the net," Spencer said. "I knew you were gonna get to the front."

"It was a sweet pass," Charlie said. He slapped his shin pads. "Of course I had to pop it off the iron — to make it interesting."

"I enjoyed watching," Dylan said.

"I enjoyed getting two gloves in my face," Pudge said. "The refs weren't gonna call anything."

"They can call it a goal," Spencer said.

The boys at the bench held their gloves out and Charlie went down the line slapping them. There were thirty-four seconds left. Charlie felt so fired up he could easily have stayed out, and Hilton had not called for a change. Charlie sensed this was another Rule Five moment, however.

"Let's change 'em," he called out, banging on the door for Zachary to open. "Take care of business, Brandon." He plonked himself down on the bench.

Zachary shut the forwards' door and slapped the top of Charlie's helmet. "Awesome possum, dude. Way to gut it out," he said.

Charlie took a sip of water. "Not sure I've ever been happier to see a puck go in."

Hilton put a hand on his shoulder. "I loved the second effort. That's what I mean about the killer instinct. They let up, and you made them pay." He gave Charlie's shoulder a tap and turned his attention to the game.

Charlie held out a glove to Pudge and they punched. "I believe that's what they call a breakout, at least around here," he said.

"I figured even you couldn't miss that open net," Pudge said.

Charlie drummed on the top of the boards. "I can miss open nets. Trust me."

Scott and Nick were leading the crowd in the countdown.

"Ten . . . Nine . . . Eight . . . Seven . . ."

Pudge leaned closer to him. "So it's just Rule Five we have to remember?" he said.

"Refer to Rule One on that — keep it simple."

". . . Three . . . Two . . . One."

"Awesome work, Rebels," Charlie yelled, springing to his feet. He exchanged high-fives all around.

"That was as much your goal as mine," he said to Spencer and they both hopped the boards to go congratulate Andrew. "You took it end to end."

Spencer tapped Charlie's shin pads with his stick. "I'm happy with the assist," he said.

Was this the Rebels' ray of light at the end of the tunnel? Everyone was excited by the last-minute goal. But how would they react to his outburst? Was it enough?

He got to the goalie and they butted heads.

"Let's keep that bargain going," Andrew said.

"What's that?"

"I won't let the puck in, and you keep scoring."

"Deal," he said, and gave the goalie a rub at the back of his head and a whack on his pads.

The Rebels' supporters gave them a nice cheer as they came off. Charlie felt relief more than anything. It was a positive step in a season with more than its share of misfortune. Matt was coming back, Zachary and Nick were in rehab and Scott should be playing in a few weeks, too.

Then he remembered the café, and had to force it from his thoughts.

Rule One — Keep it simple.

He would worry about it tomorrow.

"Rebels are on fire!" he heard Scott saying in the dressing room. He pushed the door open and whooped it up with his teammates.

10

EASY DOES IT

The Frisbee caught an updraft and flitted up suddenly. Charlie had to take three quick steps back. He timed his leap and reached with his left hand. His fingertips caught the inside lip and the disc bounced straight up. He calmly popped the Frisbee on his index finger a couple of times and in one motion brought it down and fired it to Pudge.

"Joyce-monster with the major snag," Scott proclaimed.

Nick put two fingers in his mouth and blasted an ear-piercing whistle. Jonathon, Matt and Zachary applauded also.

Charlie bowed low to the ground.

"I know it was likely the greatest catch in the history of Frisbeedom, but I don't want to talk about it," he said.

Since the bus accident, with so many of them hurt, they didn't play ball hockey that often at lunch. Instead, they had taken to tossing the Frisbee around on the field by the side of the school. Pudge lofted a floater to Julia. She bounced it several times on her finger, spun, caught it behind her back and then ripped a perfect low toss to Charlie. He did a 360 and caught it with a sweeping right hand.

"Now you're just showing off," Scott said.

Charlie threw it to him, but he wasn't paying attention and it went over his head and skidded across the pavement, ending up in the middle of a group of kids huddled by the school.

"Your pathetic throw was a disappointment," Scott said. "I used to idolize you, and now I realize how bogus you are."

"I guess it was kind of unfair for Charlie to expect you to be able to catch a Frisbee. Shame on you, Charlie," Nick said.

"Yo. Can you dudes toss the bean back?" Zachary called out.

Charlie's heart sank when Jake emerged from the group holding the Frisbee, flanked by Liam and Thomas. Jake looked at the Frisbee, reared back and let it sail. It was a beauty — but it was in the total opposite direction from the field.

"Is there a level of jerk he can't reach?" Scott said.

"I'll get it," Pudge said.

Charlie knew he needed to calm down or he would confront Jake, and then there would be a fight — and he'd seen how well that worked out.

"Chill, guys," he said. "I'll get it." He ran off before Pudge could object. Why didn't other people see Jake for what he really was? he wondered. Charlie found the Frisbee under a bush. He had to get on his knees to fish it out from under the branches. When he got up his pants were wet. "Perfect," he said out loud. He jogged back to his friends.

"When I'm King of the World and Middle Earth, I've decided I will banish Jake from the planet," Scott said.

"I'd rather let him rot in a dungeon," Nick said.

"We could put him in one of those cages that hang from the ceiling," Alexandra said.

"Like the ones where the prisoner's hands and legs stick out?" Scott said.

"Precisely," Alexandra said.

"We'll need some rats," Nick said, "and plenty of spiders."

"And once a week we might even feed him," Alexandra said.

They began to think of ways to enhance Jake's dungeon experience and the mood lightened — all except Charlie's. He could not shake his rage. Why *did* Jake get away with this stuff? he kept asking himself.

He felt a tug on his sleeve. Julia was looking at him. The rest of his friends had begun to wander back to school.

"Are you . . . did you hear me?"

"Oh. Sorry. What was that?"

She scrunched her nose to the side. "Are you ignoring me or just being spacey?"

Charlie patted his thigh with the Frisbee. "Not ignoring; definitely spacey."

"Have you been busy lately?" Julia said. "I've barely talked to you the past couple of weeks."

He saw Jake and his friends heading back to school, laughing and high-fiving. Life's a big joke, isn't it, Wilkenson? he thought.

"Charlie, this is beginning to feel like ignoring," Julia said.

Charlie flushed. "No. I . . . It isn't that. Sorry. What did you say?"

She clasped her hands behind her back. "Jake's really getting to you, isn't he," she said.

Like his mom and Pudge, Julia had this way of knowing what was going on in his head. He'd gotten used to it with Pudge. Julia doing it still freaked him out.

"Not sure it's more than usual. Or maybe he's upped his game a bit," attempting to make a joke of it.

Julia remained serious. "Some of us have been worrying about you — and the café. I can only imagine how awful it was." Her voice trailed off.

"The café will be fine."

"Okay. Good. Then that's . . . Okay. Just wondering." They turned the corner and headed to the front doors. "I heard about your fight," she said suddenly.

"It was stupid of me. Lost my cool, hurt the team; a totally dumb move."

She flicked her eyebrows. "I think some people were happy to see Jake on his butt."

"Definitely the silver lining to costing us the game."

"It didn't cost you the game. I thought it happened in the second period."

"They gave me four minutes on top of it, and Jake got two goals on the power play, and after that the team fell apart. Some of the guys were ticked off, and I can't blame them."

"You're too hard on yourself," she said quietly, and tucked her hair behind her ears. "Not everything that happens is your fault."

They joined the line-up to get in.

Charlie looked over at Jake and Liam. They were pretending to put on underarm deodorant. He began to panic.

"What are those clowns doing?" Julia said.

He had to think fast, or she would be humiliated!

"It's an old joke of theirs. It's nothing."

"Grow up," she snapped at Jake and Liam.

Liam saluted. "Right away, Ms Chow. But I need a shower first," he said, emphasizing the word shower.

That lame joke cracked them up. Jake turned his back on him and Julia, and made as if he was shampooing his hair. Charlie reckoned he was about seven metres away. Not the easiest shot, but he gripped the Frisbee tightly and let it go.

Whack.

The Frisbee smoked Jake right in the back of the head.

"Sorry. Hand must have slipped," he said.

Julia stared at Charlie, open-mouthed.

Jake rubbed his head and looked about to lose it, but then suddenly a grin spread across his face.

"There's an expression I've been saving for a special occasion like this. Do you wanna hear it?"

"Not particularly," Charlie said.

"You should: When you ride a tiger, you ride forever. Which means it's easy to start something, but you can't always decide who finishes it. In this case, that'll be me."

"Big talk, as usual."

The mood had become so tense that a crowd began to gather, forming a semi-circle around them. His friends had already gone in, which meant he was on his own. He looked over at his rival. Jake and he had been linked since the first day he came here. He and his crew had made it hard on Charlie, always ready to tear him down, always trying to make him look bad He had thrown the Frisbee because they were dissing Julia. But now, as he stood there, alone, Jake and his friends laughing at him, the surrounding students waiting eagerly for a fight, he realized there was more to it. He was sick of Jake and how he made him feel, sick of the trash-talking, the taunts, the threats.

"Bring it, Tiger," Charlie said.

Jake rolled his neck, his eyes ablaze, and stepped toward Charlie. Charlie braced himself, trying to clear his head. Jake was a big dude, and no slouch with his fists. He would have to be ready for anything.

"Do him in, Jake," Liam said.

"Pound the loser," Thomas said.

Jake sneered. "Hold still. That way it'll be less painful." He began to bob and weave in exaggerated fashion, to the great delight of this friends and the crowd, many of whom cheered and laughed at his antics. But it occurred to Charlie that Jake was actually paying more attention to the crowd than to him, too busy showing off. If he made his move now he could get in the first shot. He readied himself.

Julia stepped in between them. "This is stupid. Enough," she said. "You two have been at each other since grade nine. And why?"

With Julia in the way he could not get at Jake, and Jake had backed up anyway, his arms to his sides and his fists open, no longer looking like he wanted to fight. That mocking half smile he always used when dissing

Charlie almost sent him over the edge, it was so infuriating. Frustrated by the lost opportunity, Charlie felt angry at Julia, as if she had cheated him from settling things.

"Joyce, I knew you were a total wuss, but I gotta admit that Chow here scares me. No way I'm fightin' her." He sniffed the air. "Besides, there's a rotten banana or something around here. I'm splittin'."

Julia shook her head. "What's with you?"

"Nothin'," Jake said. "I'm just gonna go inside. Something's bothering my nose. Might be my allergies."

"I will join you, Mr. Wilkenson. There is something odd in the air ," Liam said, barely covering up his laughter. "Toodles, Char-Char." Roscoe and Thomas laughed outright.

The crowd began to drift away. Jake blew them a kiss and bumped fists with Roscoe and Thomas. Both of them roared at something Jake said, and then they disappeared into the school.

Soon Charlie and Julia were alone.

"Are you going to tell me what they're up to? I know it's something to do with me," Julia said.

Charlie's frustration slowly disappeared. Maybe she had butted into his business by stopping the fight; but then again, a fight might have gotten him in serious trouble with the school and it would not have solved anything. When would he ever learn? Every time he lost it with them he ended up looking dumb. Besides, he had to admire her bravery. It could not have been easy for her to jump in between two angry boys.

Charlie took a deep breath and gave his shoulders a

shrug on the exhale. He was still jacked up from the close encounter with Jake. "They're being themselves — jerks," Charlie said slowly. "It's an old routine of theirs — they are suggesting . . . my showering habits could be better." He prayed she believed him.

Julia did not answer immediately, but soon she allowed herself a smile. She gave Charlie's shoulder a light punch. "I still think fighting is totally ridiculous — but for what it's worth I know you would've taken him."

Charlie was not so sure, and he was willing to bet she was not really either, but it was nice to hear her say it anyway. The bell rang, and they walked over to the school. He opened the door and followed her in.

"Can I trust you to go through the rest of the afternoon without starting another fracas?" she said, a slight smile lighting up her eyes.

"I'll be a good boy — for today, at least."

"Not exactly the answer I was looking for but I'll take it. See you later."

"See you, Julia." He paused. Should he thank her for sticking up for him? It might sound like he was actually afraid to face Jake straight on, though, and the idea of a girl defending him in a fight was embarrassing.

Before he decided, Julia pushed through the inner doors and was gone. It was with some relief that he watched her head down the hallway, and it occurred to him that just as he had been connected with Jake since he came to Terrence Falls, so too had he been connected with Julia.

11

STRESS TEST

Bang!

Charlie smashed his combination lock against his locker. "Total waste of twenty minutes," he muttered. He had forgotten his knapsack in history class and had to find the janitor to unlock the room. And he had to get back home in time to get Danielle and Hannah to their drama class.

Bang!

It was probably pointless, but another combo smash against the locker made him feel better, and he raced off down the stairs. He burst through the double doors and turned left toward his house. Pudge, Scott, Nick and Zachary were milling around outside. Pudge waved.

"Toss the bean," he called out.

"Hi, guys," he said. "I forgot my bag in a classroom, and had to find —"

"We know. You forgot something and then forgot something else and then misplaced something and now you can't find it or remember what you were looking for, and, of course, now you're late," Scott said.

"Let's at least toss the bean around now that Jake's not here," Pudge said.

"About the Frisbee," Charlie said tentatively. "I think Jake might have it. I might've thrown it at his head."

"Perhaps we could get the back story on that," Zachary said.

He told them quickly, leaving out the part about Julia.

"Jake stole my Frisbee?" Pudge said.

"It appears so," Charlie said.

"I'm gonna miss that Frisbee," Scott said. "It was round and circular . . . and round."

"And it was round," Nick said.

"Gotta run, guys," Charlie said. "I'm late. Gotta take my sister and her friend to a drama class, and a few other things to do. Sorry. Catch you at the game tonight. Huge game. We beat the Snow Birds and the Rebels are back in business."

Charlie dropped his long board to the ground and pushed off as fast as he could go. The whirring of the wheels was usually a comfort. This time it made him more anxious because he could not make them go any faster. It had been less than two weeks since his mom had started her baking business, and it was as if his entire life had changed overnight. His mom was out of the house by three-thirty or four in the morning now, and she was in bed by nine o'clock at night, sometimes earlier. That meant Charlie was making breakfast and lunch, for himself and Danielle, plus doing laundry, plus taking Danielle to her drama and hockey, plus putting out the garbage and the recycling, plus doing house-cleaning. Danielle helped out a bit, but most of the work fell on his shoulders.

As he pushed his way up the hill to his house he tried to work out a strategy. First, make sure Danny eats her sandwich. Second, over to Hannah's house, and then walk them to drama class. The class was an hour, so he would have time to get home and eat before his game. Then back to pick up the girls — and pray they were not late like last time or did not fool around too much on the way home. Pudge's dad was supposed to pick him up at eight. He should be back in time, and if he got lucky he might have twenty minutes to work on his science homework. He also had to fold the laundry. It had been sitting there for two days, and his mom had left him a note about it this morning.

He was not complaining — if this meant they stayed in Terrence Falls than he was happy to do it — but still, it was exhausting just thinking about all that.

* * *

He slammed the front door behind him. "Next time you've got to get ready faster," Charlie said.

"You told me that about twelve hundred thousand times," Danielle said, "and your stupid hockey game isn't my problem."

"Thanks. Really appreciate that after rushing around like a madman to get you to your drama class. Why is *your* drama class *my* problem?"

"It wasn't my fault that the class was long. We were working on something."

"Don't give me that. You were messing around with Hannah."

She stomped off. Charlie forced himself to unclench his fists. Mom could deal with her now.

"Hey, mom. Danny's home. I'm off to hockey," he

called out. There was no answer. She must be sleeping already. He peered out the window. It was getting late. Pudge's dad had better get here soon or they would be late, and he did not need that on top of everything else. He looked out again. Where *was* he?

A fretful five minutes later he saw headlights turning into the driveway. Finally! He pulled the door open, held the knob for a moment, and then closed it. Even though his sister had been beyond irritating, he was starting to feel a little bad about getting so mad at her. He ran to the kitchen. "If you need anything to eat, there's that half a sandwich in the fridge, and there's a piece of chocolate cake too. I'm going to my game." He paused slightly, and added, "And I'm sorry for yelling at you. I'm just stressed. We're playing the Snow Birds and it's a big game. We really need this one." Then he noticed the chocolate cake and sandwich in front of her.

"Poor Charlie," she said. "You always make yourself crazy." She yawned and with her elbows on the table leaned her head into her right hand.

Classic Danielle. Just when you wanted to kill her, she made you laugh. "You're right about that. Mom's sleeping, so you'll have to go to bed on your own. Not too late, either. Nine-thirty at the latest."

She screwed her eyes tight and scrunched her mouth to one side. "Mom's not here, crazy one."

The doorbell rang.

Charlie stared at his sister. "What? That's impossible. She said to me she'd be back by seven-thirty at the latest." He looked over at the stove. It was 8:10.

"I checked her bedroom. Nada."

The doorbell rang again. He groaned and went to the door.

"Mr. Joyce. I know you love the thrill of being late, but I have a reputation to uphold," Pudge said.

Charlie's mind was racing. "This is a nightmare. My mom's not here . . . I can't . . . Danielle is here . . ."

Pudge turned pale. "But we gotta go."

"Hold on a sec. I'll call her cell." He ran back to the kitchen and punched at the dial pad feverishly. "Answer. Answer."

"You've reached the Rainbow Café. Please leave a message and . . ."

He jabbed the End button and redialled. Again, he got her voicemail.

"What's going on, dude?" Pudge called out.

"I'm calling my mom . . . No answer." He closed his eyes. His mom was bound to be home soon. Danielle was ten . . . She could be on her own for a few minutes . . . half an hour . . . couldn't she? He had promised Hilton and the guys he would not be late again . . . and not against the first-place Snow Birds . . . But he'd promised his mom too. He looked over at Danielle. She had polished off the cake and was chomping into her sandwich. His stomach felt like it had shrunk into a tiny ball. He ran back to Pudge.

"I've gotta wait for my mom. You go. Tell Hilton I'll be there soon. My mom must've gotten held up for some reason."

Pudge looked like he did not understand him. "It's the Snow Birds. You can't miss the game. I mean . . . maybe I'll watch Danielle. Without you covering J.C. Savard we'll get killed."

A more loyal teammate and friend never existed. Pudge was willing to miss the game so he could play. But Charlie could not live with that. This was his problem, not Pudge's. "No, it's okay. She'll be back soon and she can drive me. You get there and tell Hilton what happened — and tell him I'm sorry. It must be serious if she's late."

Pudge stared at Charlie and then looked away. The horn blasted twice. "Okay. I'll call you when I get to the rink. And if your mom can't drive for some reason, call my cell and my Dad will come back and get you."

"It'll be fine. Get going. I'll see you soon," Charlie said.

Pudge hesitated briefly, then held out his fist for Charlie to give it a punch and ran down the stairs to the van. Charlie watched it back up and pull away. He went to the kitchen. It was 8:14 The game was at 9:20. Pudge would be lucky if he got there an hour ahead. Charlie slumped into a chair.

Brutal. Brutal. Brutal.

Danielle had finished her sandwich and was mixing a glass of chocolate milk. "Are you not going to play tonight?" she said.

Charlie ignored the nausea rising to his throat. "I will. As soon as Mom gets back, I'll go."

She slid her chocolate milk toward him. "Want some? It's the best thing for energy."

"You drink chocolate milk after playing, not before."

She shrugged. "Don't blame me when you get tired in the third period."

Charlie did not feel like talking. He quickly dialled

his mom again. Same thing. He was going to miss this game. The new Rebels would just love that; even his buds would be ticked off — and all this after his big-shot speech during the Flames game!

He was driving himself nuts. He needed something to take his mind off the situation. He spotted his knap-sack. May as well get some homework done while he waited. He pulled out his science textbook and his notes. The words on the page were a blur. Now his eye-sight was going! He looked over at the clock again: 8:18. Back to his work. He managed to focus a bit bet-ter and work through a problem.

"I'm gonna watch TV until bed," Danielle said.

Charlie's heart set to pounding again. "Yeah. Sure. Go ahead." He checked the time: 8:30. He had a weird sensation of having to both go to the washroom and throw up. He moved on to the next problem.

Ring. Ring. Ring.

Charlie's heart nearly blasted through his chest. He almost wished time would just jump ahead and the game be over. He was going to have a heart attack! He reached for the phone.

"Charlie. Any news?"

Pudge.

"Not yet."

"I can't believe this. We need you. Have you called her again? "

"I did. Left a bunch of messages. How's Hilton?"

"Not happy. Talk to ya."

He hung up. The next science problem made no sense to him. The numbers seemed all mixed up. He gave his head a shake and went at it again. Maybe he should skip this one. But the next problem wasn't clear either. He couldn't even think.

Ring. Ring. Ring.

At least this time he didn't freak out. Pudge was only trying to help, but he was not in the mood to talk to him. It made him feel worse.

"Still nothing, Pudge."

"Charlie, it's Mom."

Charlie's stomach tightened back into a tight ball. "Hi, Mom . . . is everything . . . okay?"

"I'm so sorry, Charlie. I lost track of time. There was a disaster today. One of Bruno's cooks turned the oven up and a huge order was ruined. He didn't know I had stuff in there, or I didn't make it clear, at least that's what he said . . . doesn't matter . . . Anyway, I had to start over and on top of that get things prepped for tomorrow morning — and with all the stress I forgot about your game. Honey, I'm so sorry. I don't know what to say."

"So . . . that's it then. You can't come . . . I could call Pudge's dad to get me . . . but I feel bad about it . . . I should, though . . ."

"Don't bother. I'm done, and I'm five minutes away. I'll be there."

Charlie put his books away. Now he was ten times more nervous. Best-case scenario was to get there by about ten after nine. He could get dressed in five minutes no problem. Hopefully, he would be ready for the warm-up. He collected Danielle's dishes and put them into the dishwasher. She could help out more. He felt like he was picking up after her all day. And she had left crumbs all over the counter. His mom hated a dirty counter. Charlie wet a cloth and wiped it down.

"Hey, Danielle," he called out downstairs. "You wanna come for a drive with me and mom for a minute to the rink? She's gonna give me a lift."

The television turned off, and he heard her feet shuffling up the stairs. That was a relief. He thought she would want to stay home, and put up a fight.

"Thanks, D," he said.

"You owe me, dude," she said.

Despite it all he had to laugh. "I'll try to make it up to you," he said.

12

SQUARE ONE

J. C. Savard, the Snow Birds' star centre, wheeled with the puck in the neutral zone. Charlie came at him from the side boards, angry at himself for losing track of Savard and allowing a simple pass from a defenceman to fool him. He stretched his stick out. Savard evaded the weak effort easily and, flanked by his wingers, bore down on the twins. Edging toward Robert, he slid the puck to his left winger, then swerved in that direction in support. Robert had to backpedal under the pressure, and the puck carrier gained the blue line. Charlie urged his tired legs to work harder. A burning in his thighs acted like a giant weight on his back. He felt as if he were skating through mud, as he had the entire game.

The right winger drove wide and then took it inside about two metres from the high slot. Robert pushed off his right edge, his left shoulder lowered. It was a foolish decision, coming across the middle against those two defencemen. Robert took a step forward, readying for the hit. Charlie slowed, confident Robert would erase the threat. The winger had other ideas. The puck on his forehand, he dipped his left shoulder and sent a no-look backhander to Savard sneaking in on the right side. The twins had collapsed to cut the winger off, and Savard had a clear path on goal. The winger sidestepped Robert's intended hit and cut hard on his inside edges to continue on to the net, Christopher struggling to hold him up.

The slick centre dangled the puck in front of Andrew, took two steps across the top of the crease, and then brought it back to his forehand. Andrew dropped and threw out his left pad. Savard hesitated ever so slightly, and with a flick of the wrists roofed it over his outstretched glove and into the top corner. That made it 6–1 for the Snow Birds, with ten minutes left to play in the third. It was Savard's second goal to add to an assist.

Charlie continued back with his stick across his shin pads and stopped beside his goaltender.

"I'm officially depressed," Martin said. "Does that guy ever get tired of making me look useless?"

"That was my bad," Charlie said. "Stupid play at their blue line, and I let Savard get away from me."

"We gotta get some pressure on them," Martin said. "We've had like ten shots all game. This is embarrassing."

Charlie tapped Martin's pads. "Hang tough. We'll get through this."

Martin thrust his blocker and glove on top of his pads and bounced a few times. Charlie did not push it. No goalie likes to get blitzed, especially when he feels his team has let him down, and there was no doubt the Rebels had left Martin to face the mighty Snow Birds virtually on his own.

Charlie made his way to the bench. He could feel

Hilton's icy stare. Savard had scorched him today. Charlie had been on the ice for all but one of the Snow Birds' goals. Dylan had counted the only marker for the Rebels back in the first period, off a sweet setup by Spencer and Brandon. Charlie sneaked a glance at his teammates. All had long faces, slumped shoulders, hanging heads — a defeated team.

Charlie had arrived at the arena five minutes before the game started, missing the warm-up and his first shift. He felt like a house-leaguer waiting at the door for a stoppage in play so he could sneak to the bench. His teammates did not seem to care too much and they were obviously glad he made it; even Spencer cracked a joke about it. Hilton was a different story, but after Charlie explained he seemed to accept it.

Given the mood on the bench, the score and his lateness, Charlie decided another rousing speech from the captain was definitely a bad idea. This was a game to get over with, and maybe they could try to score another goal to at least end it on a less depressing note. But it wasn't a leadership moment, as far as he saw it.

Charlie watched on as, for one of the rare times this game, the Rebels had the Snow Birds hemmed in their own end. Brandon and Will were cycling the puck effectively on the right side. Nazem joined in the effort, and he sent a crisp pass to Spencer at the point. The Snow Birds were a poised team, however. The left winger had not strayed too far down, and he was able to force Spencer to hammer the puck back down the wall. Brandon pressed his left leg against the boards to stop it before it went behind the net. They began to cycle again, with the Snow Birds defenders giving them the outside, and steadfastly preventing them from penetrating inside.

"That's how you play defence," Hilton said. "No panic. Stay in your position. Play hard and wait for a giveaway. Take note."

Charlie took a sip of water. "We need to do more of that. Wear their defence down. Let's get the puck and cycle next shift," he said to Pudge.

"I'm sitting one out," Pudge said.

He should have known that.

"Charlie's up next with Jonathon and Dylan," Hilton barked. "Be ready. They'll be tired. It's been a long shift."

Charlie took another sip of water and spit it onto the ice. He would never say it out loud, but he envied Pudge missing a shift. His legs still had that dead feeling. His energy level had been close to zero the entire game, which was bizarre for him. Usually, he was too hyped to sit still and he was always jumping up to yell one thing or another. Charlie had been waiting for his energy to come since the first period. He looked at the clock. Eight minutes to go.

Brandon had the puck on the half boards, and he found Spencer at the top of the circle. The left winger had not lost focus and he deflected the shot as it came off Spencer's stick. The puck flew over the net and into the netting. The referee blew the play down and pointed to the faceoff dot to the goaltender's left. Charlie stepped onto the ice.

"Great work, Rebels," he said to his teammates as they came off to change. He slapped Brandon's pads.

Nobody responded.

He couldn't blame them — it was hard to get

stoked because of one good shift when you were getting smoked. Charlie adopted a reverse grip and hunched over for the draw, happy that Savard was not on for this shift. But just as he was getting comfortable, a tall, broad-shouldered defenceman slipped in front of the Snow Birds right winger. It was nice to have Savard off, but this defenceman was Burnett, and he was the Snow Birds' other superstar. He was almost as dangerous as Savard. Charlie would have to watch him. The referee blew his whistle, held the puck over the dot and dropped it. Charlie slid his right foot forward and swept at the puck, carrying through with his right shoulder into the other centre.

He groaned. Another lost draw. He had barely won any all game. The left defenceman banked the puck behind the net and off the wall to Burnett, who took it on his forehand and started up ice. The centre thrust his stick into Charlie's ribs and pushed off to his right, leaving him gasping for air. The quickness of the play forced Robert to back off, and once again the Snow Birds were off and running — with Charlie caught watching.

Burnett headmanned the puck to the right winger. Their left winger swung into the middle of the neutral zone and accepted a soft pass, with his centre sliding into his spot on the boards. He was rewarded for his efforts with a backhand pass. Jonathon had decided to stay with the left winger and Dylan cut over to cover the right side. Charlie put his head down and kept pushing to come back. Not again, he prayed.

The good news was the centre did not score. The bad news was he crossed the Rebels' blue line, froze Christopher by selling an outside move, and hit Burnett trailing into the high slot. Burnett took two more steps, raised his stick high over his shoulder and let a blazing slapshot go. A huge cheer sounded from the stands. Burnett held his arms over his head. Charlie put his stick across his shin pads and dropped his head. Another goal.

Brandon's line came on. Charlie dropped next to Pudge on the bench and reached for a water bottle. He felt a presence behind him.

"Losing the draw I can live with. But letting the centre push you aside like a little boy, and giving him ten metres because you decided to watch the play is not acceptable," Hilton said. "Rule Three — Keep your feet moving. That starts the second the puck is dropped, not when we give up an odd-man rush."

Hilton walked away. Charlie hit his helmet with the shaft of his stick. Moronic play. Too busy admiring Burnett to cover the centre. Hilton was right. He had been a step behind the entire game. He felt a glove tap his knee.

"Not our night," Pudge said.

"I've been useless," Charlie said.

"No one's had a great game."

"I think Savard's using a magic spell to control me. It's the only reasonable explanation."

"Next line is Dylan at centre, with Jonathon and Pudge," Hilton announced.

Charlie slumped his shoulders. He and Brandon were always the centres. Hilton was really upset with him. Given how he felt, maybe missing one shift was not the worst thing. He took a long sip of water. About thirty seconds later, after another nice shift spent mostly in the Snow Birds' end, Brandon, Will and Nazem shifted.

Brandon sat next to Charlie.

"Are you hurt? How come you're sitting?" Brandon said.

Charlie was not going to lie. "I think Hilton's sending me a message."

Brandon looked back on the ice. Spencer lifted the stick of an attacking forward, stole the puck and sent a cross-ice pass to Jonathon on the right side.

"He's had a good game," Brandon said.

Charlie agreed. Spencer had not given up for a second, and had been all over the ice. Probably the Rebels' best player tonight.

"Brandon's line is up next," Hilton said.

Dylan and Pudge had done nicely on the left side with a bit of cycling, and a smart pass from Philip to Spencer and then to Jonathon down low had resulted in a great scoring chance. Only a quick glove-hand save prevented a goal. The Rebels changed on the fly and Charlie moved over.

No point worrying about the past. He had one or maybe two shifts left. Enough time to prove what he was made of. This time he even wanted Savard to be out there. He was going to shut him down, and Burnett, and anyone else. He was going to outwork them all.

"Great shift," he said to his linemates as they came off. "Beautiful cycling, Pudge, Dylan — and nice shot, Jonathon. He robbed you. Total luck."

"I want the same line out next," Hilton said. "That was a good effort."

"The cycling game is working," Charlie continued,

as if nothing was out of the ordinary. "Let's get one back. Forget the score. Just get one."

No one responded.

And this moment was anything but ordinary.

He was not getting those last shifts.

Charlie Joyce had been benched for the rest of the game.

13

DIG DEEP

He awoke with a start.

"Charlie. Charlie."

His mom shook him again. Charlie slowly raised his head from the pillow, rubbing his eyes. "What was . . . What time is it? . . . What . . .?"

"I need you to wake up," his mom said sternly. "It's ten-thirty."

He gave his head a little shake and blinked a few more times to clear the cobwebs. "I'm up. What's wrong?"

"What's wrong is I have a special order, a wedding cake, and I couldn't do it at the restaurant, so I have to do it here. Only you didn't pick up the flour, eggs and butter like I asked, and you didn't help Danielle with her project, not to mention that you didn't put your laundry away. I've been working since four in the morning, Charlie, and I needed those things done."

He couldn't argue. She was dead right. Only he still felt tired, and would have loved to roll over and go back to sleep. The Snow Birds game had not ended until after ten-thirty, and by the time he had changed, showered, agonized, sulked and worried — and then agonized, sulked, and worried some more — it had been after midnight.

"I'll get going. No worries. I don't have hockey today. What do I need to buy again?"

"Forget about that. I took care of it. But I need you to run to the Rainbow and get my wedding cake book under the counter by the cash. I'm totally under the gun. I need to get that cake out by five o'clock. I also need my piping bags for the icing. They're in a drawer next to the bread oven. I'm just praying they weren't ruined by the fire." She ran her fingers through her hair. "A wedding cake in seven hours. One mistake and I'm done for."

"You can do it, Mom. I've seen your cakes."

She smiled weakly. "I appreciate your confidence. You can take your time a bit — but I need it in an hour. I can get started on the batter, but I'll need the other stuff after that."

Charlie threw the covers off and reached for his pants on the floor. His mom rolled her eyes. "Ordinarily, I'd give you a mini-lecture about leaving your stuff all over the place, but since it'll get you out the door faster, I'll keep it to myself."

Charlie put his pants on quickly. His mom held out a set of keys, which he stuffed into his pocket.

"How was the game? Did you win?" she said.

"Don't ask. We got pounded — and I played like garbage."

"I can't believe it was that bad."

"Trust me. I'm insulting garbage by comparing myself to it." He let his arms dangle by his sides. He really was tired. "I had no energy. Maybe cause I didn't get a warm-up, not sure. I couldn't get into the game. I was like a minus six on the night." He swallowed hard. "I even got benched."

His mom squeezed his arm. "You're working hard, and I know this has been difficult for you. I shouldn't get on you so much. I'm sorry. We're both trying to do a whole bunch of things at the same time, and we're going to make mistakes, like me last night and you this morning."

"I'm sorry too, Mom. I tell myself ten times a night to set my alarm, and then I forget. How dumb is that?" He buttoned up his shirt and pulled on his sweatshirt.

She sat on his bed, then leaned down to pick up a towel and fold it. "I got another call from Theresa," she said. "She needs an answer from me by the end of the year, which is only about five weeks away, or she'll have to find someone else."

"So let her find someone."

"Charlie . . ." She seemed to be searching for words. "I'd love to. Believe me. It's just that . . . it's that I'm worried about you, and us. I spoke to my lawyer and, well, she's telling me this is going to take a long time. The insurance company won't budge. We're running out of money. I can't go on like this; even a couple more months will be very hard. I'm drawing on savings now, and I'm not sure it's worth it. Things are too hectic, especially for you. You've got big circles under your eyes. It's not healthy. And I'm getting worn out too. And how long can I work at the restaurant? Bruno's been lovely to me, but I'm getting in the way. I've been looking into renting another kitchen space, but it's so expensive and places are hard to find."

"Are you saying we have to go?"

She swayed slowly from side to side. "I'm saying we have to think about it and be prepared for it. Unless I can find another kitchen that's affordable — soon — and business picks up enough that I can hire some help again, it just won't work, honey. I hate the thought of moving you and Danny. But money is so tight right now, and this job in Stanville will take the pressure off. It really is a fantastic opportunity."

Charlie stared out the window.

"I'm not saying it's for sure," she continued, "but like I said, I don't want to surprise you . . ."

He interrupted her, the words pouring out. "I won't forget stuff again, Mom. I swear. This was only because we had a late game — and so what if I miss a game once in a while. So what. I don't want to move because you feel sorry for me. I'm good. Everything's good. I don't feel stressed. Honest. I just forgot to set the alarm. No biggie. And I'll ride to the Rainbow and get your book in two secs — and I'm happy to help Danny with her project. I'll tell her before I go. I'm in all day doing my homework anyway, so there's no problem, and you're the best baker in Terrence Falls and you'll get tons of work. I know it. And I'm sure your lawyer will get the money to fix up the Rainbow soon."

His mom got up. "You're probably right, Charlie. I'm tired too, and stressed about this wedding cake. That's all. It'll probably work out. Don't worry." But she did not sound convinced.

He crossed his arms. "Do you need anything else?"

"No. That's it."

"Okay. I'll see you in, like, five minutes."

"You don't have to kill yourself, Charlie. I don't need it till the batter's ready. Do you want to eat something quick before you go?"

"I'm not really hungry," he said. "I'll eat when I come back."

He took a quick look again out the window. The sky had darkened. He grabbed his knapsack and his board. "Like I said, I'll be back quick. Bye." He ran downstairs. The television was on. "Hey, Danny. Do you want me to help with your project later?"

"Nah. Mom will do it," she called up from the basement.

"Mom's got to bake a wedding cake. I can help."

She didn't answer for a moment. "Okay. Later, though. I want to see the end of this."

"Not a problem." He was out the door in a flash and riding down the street as fast as he could. His stomach began to rumble. A little food might have been a good idea. In fact, now he almost felt sick to his stomach, he was so hungry. Two more pushes and he got up to top speed, and only then noticed the car at the stop sign. Charlie pushed the back wheels forward, and with knees bent deeply, leaned back. For a second he thought he might have to ditch. Another metre and he would have smashed into the side door.

He waved at the driver and gave him a thumbs-up. The driver gave him a stern look before pulling off. Charlie waited for his heart to stop pounding like a drum. At least that woke him up! The intersection was clear, so he set off again, a little more cautiously this time.

* * *

A strand of police tape remained in front of the café, flapping in the wind. The front window had been covered up with paper. Charlie unlocked the door and turned on the lights. The sight of the damage brought the memories flooding back, and for a few moments he allowed himself to remember that night.

He sat down on a chair.

He might have to leave Terrence Falls.

And then, for the first time since his father died, Charlie cried.

Pounding on the front door startled him so much he nearly fell off the chair.

"Who's there?" he called.

The pounding continued.

"Who is it?"

He heard a muffled yell outside. He thought he heard his name. Quickly, Charlie wiped his eyes. Then he dimmed the lights and peeked through a crack in the paper. Pudge was staring back at him. He prayed Pudge would not notice that he had been crying. But what was he doing here? Charlie opened the door.

"Hey, Charlie. We went by your house and your Mom told us you'd just left. We figured we'd meet you," Pudge said.

Dalton and Matt came in.

Charlie touched the corner of his right eye nonchalantly. It felt dry.

"We're going over to Zachary's to watch the hockey game," Pudge said.

"It's not tonight?" Charlie said, blinking a few times. His eyes felt dry, but he dared not touch them again.

"A rare matinee," Dalton said.

"I can't. Not right now, anyway. I have to get a cookbook to my mom, and then help Danielle with some work, and I have homework to do . . . maybe I can come for the third period . . ."

"Charlie Joyce is choosing homework over a hockey game?" Matt said. "Did I just see a pig fly by?"

"I've never seen you so busy with school before," Pudge said. "You trying to be the new Matt?"

Little chance of that happening. Matt was the school genius — well, one of them. Julia was the other one.

Dalton began to look around. "This was truly an unfortunate event," he said. "Do you know how it started?"

Charlie felt himself flush. He had kept that a secret, except for telling Pudge. It was too embarrassing. But he couldn't bring himself to lie now. "Unfortunately, I do. I was making a grilled cheese sandwich, and Jake and his crew came over and I forgot about it and when my mom honked the horn I went out. Stuff caught on fire."

"When are you starting to fix it?" Pudge said.

"Not sure," Charlie said. "The insurance company won't give us the money." If they only knew what that meant, he thought.

"But they must provide the funds to repair the damage," Dalton said. "That's the point of insurance, no?"

Charlie had to laugh. "They say I'm underage and had no right to use the range, and the fire system wasn't turned on."

"Why was that?" Pudge said.

Charlie shrugged. "It's complicated. My mom's seeing a lawyer. It's a total mess. The guys that installed it did it wrong. Bottom line is no money. And my mom owes the bank 'cause she borrowed to start the café and . . . Like I said, a total mess."

"It is typical for a small business to finance the start up by borrowing funds," Dalton said. "I can see how it would be difficult to meet the monthly payments without a source of income. Is your mother working?"

Until that moment, Charlie had been keeping Stanville a secret. Somehow that made it less real, less like it could happen. But keeping the secret made him feel bad, as if he was lying to his buddies. He would not want his friends to keep something like this from him. As hard as it was to admit, Stanville was becoming a real possibility, and he was tired of pretending everything was fine — because it totally was not.

He started slowly, trying to think of the best way to tell them. "She's working at Pudge's dad's restaurant. She's started a baking business. It's been going okay, but not great . . . and she doesn't think it'll pick up fast enough, so . . . yeah, I think she's stressed. We all are. I've been running around a lot, helping out more at home, so it's not all homework — although I could definitely do more of that."

They all laughed, although Charlie sensed it was more to relieve the tension than because it was funny.

"Do you mind if I take a look at the damage?" Dalton said.

"Help yourself," he said, and Dalton wandered to the back. Matt followed him.

Charlie put a foot on the chair and rested an elbow

on his knee. "This was supposed to be the dream season," he said to Pudge. "Then the school hockey team is cancelled and we miss the Champions Cup, and a bus we're on goes into the lake — I mean, really, a lake? — and a bunch of guys are hurt. Now this? We should hire a witch doctor to get rid of the black cloud over our heads. Or better yet, I should leave, and you guys will be free of my curse."

"We'll get through it," Pudge said.

"I'm not so sure. My mom's been working like crazy and . . . she can't be at your dad's place forever. She got offered a new job and . . ." Charlie could not say it.

"So that's good. She can make some money and open the café again down the road," Pudge pressed. "You should be happy."

"The job's in Stanville. We'd have to move."

Pudge did not seem to react. Had he understood?

"It's not for sure or anything," Charlie said. "Hopefully, she can find another kitchen to work out of and everything will be okay."

"But my dad's happy for her to stay."

"Yeah. I know. She wants her own place, I guess. She'd have to hire people, get more business . . ."

Dalton rejoined them. "It wouldn't take too much to repair the range," Dalton said. "The handles and knobs are easy enough. The manufacturer would have those. Slightly more complicated is replacing the motherboard, which melted during the fire. I'm sure I could find something inexpensive on the internet."

"What's the point?" Charlie said. "Look at this place."

Dalton's brow furrowed and he pursed his lips. "It might be a lot of work, but if we cleaned everything up, painted, and repaired the range, this café could be up and running again."

"That's going to be someone else's problem," Charlie said.

Pudge's eyes were bright and his cheeks flushed. "If the café was fixed your mom wouldn't have to think of leaving."

"Who's leaving?" Matt said.

"No one," Charlie said. He sighed and added, "Well, maybe I am."

"Where are you going?" Dalton said.

"I'm not . . . Well, I'm probably not . . . Here's the story: Without the insurance money, my mom can't reopen the café, and if her new business doesn't pick up . . . a lot . . . we might have to leave Terrence Falls. She got offered another job at a restaurant — in Stanville."

"Then I guess we gotta fix this place," Matt said.

"If we do it, there'd be no reason to go," Pudge said.

"It's a nice idea, but think about it. We can't fix this mess," Charlie said. "We have no money. What good is a range when the rest of the place looks like this? The ceiling and walls are trashed.

"Maybe not as bad as that," Dalton said. "From what I can see the damage was principally from the smoke, a lot of which can simply be cleaned up. It is true that materials will need to be replaced — such as some of the drywall and the affected ceiling tiles, and I do see some discoloured floor tiles — but otherwise, it's not as disastrous, or 'trashed,' as you suggest."

"So you're saying it's less than a disaster?" Charlie said.

"Yes, I suppose I am."

Pudge was flushed and breathing heavily. "We'll do it ourselves," he announced.

"I . . . um . . . kinda lost my magic wand, so I'm not really sure that's possible," Charlie said.

"If we can survive the Champions Cup team last year and make it to the finals, start the Rebels, and even save the school, we can do this. We don't need your wand."

"I have an idea for construction materials," Dalton said. "My family is quite committed to the freecycling movement. People list things they don't need, new or used, on a website, and offer it free to others. I could send out a query to the local group."

Pudge raised his fist in the air. "Perfect. We freecycle this sucker back to its original glory."

"Also, my father is in real estate and he generally knows who is renovating their properties," Dalton said. "That's another terrific source of materials. Environmental types call it salvaging. You wouldn't believe what people throw out when they're fixing up their houses."

"My dad will be able to help on the advice side," Matt said.

"What does he do?" Dalton said.

"He's a carpenter — but he can build practically anything," Matt said.

"I appreciate what you're trying to do," Charlie said. "It's a cool idea, and I'd do anything to try to stay in Terrence Falls, but we don't know how to replace walls and ceilings and tiles and motherboards and . . ."

Charlie looked into his friends' eyes, and his voice grew quiet. "There's more to it. It's not actually just the repairs we have to deal with. The bank is asking for some money, and I'm not sure how much time we have."

"I think tomorrow morning we have an appointment with a certain bank manager," Pudge said.

"I'll send an SOS to the freecycling community," Dalton said, "and talk to my father."

"I'll get my dad to come over and tell us what to do," Matt said.

"Once you're done with your sister, come over to Zachary's for a planning session," Pudge said.

Charlie struggled to speak. "This is . . . I . . . um . . . will have to speak to my mom . . . " He tried to collect his thoughts. Could they actually do it?

Pudge put out his hand. Matt laid his on top, and then Dalton. Charlie added his.

"Rainbow Café on three," Pudge said.

"One–Two–Three!"

14

SUPERHERO

The wind chilled him as he rode his board toward the bank. He blew on his hands and resigned himself to the suffering. He had told his mom that morning about the plan. "It sounds rather ambitious," she had said. "I don't want you getting your hopes up." Hardly the reaction he expected, but maybe it made sense. She probably didn't want to get her own hopes up, and she did not know about their idea to go to the bank. Something about the way she had responded made him think it would be better not to tell her until the bank actually gave her an extension. She would get stoked then.

Pudge and he took the turn on their boards side by side.

"I'm hoping the cold weather won't mean a frosty reception," Charlie said. "What time is our appointment?"

"Ten-thirty."

He had asked Pudge three times already. He was totally uptight and he needed to chill. This was big, though. His mom had been talking to his grandmother on the phone, and although he felt guilty about eavesdropping, he had heard his mom say that the next bank payment was due after New Year's, which was a little over four weeks from now, and they were hounding her already for the last payment, which she had missed. He had to convince the manager to give her more time. Then they could do the repairs, she would reopen and make the money and . . . He stopped himself. He had been repeating the same thing over and over since Pudge had come up with the idea. It was enough already; now he needed to make it happen.

They stopped at a red light and picked up their boards.

"I'm freezin', dude," Charlie said. "This light better change or I might not make it. I gotta get some warmth on me."

As if the light was listening, it changed, and the two boys ran across the intersection and into the bank.

"Can I help you, gentlemen?" a lady asked.

"We have an appointment with . . . what's her name again?" Charlie asked Pudge.

"Ms Sarah Martins — for ten-thirty," Pudge said.

"Certainly. Please have a seat. She'll be with you shortly.

Charlie looked around. "I don't see any chairs."

"Around the corner there's a waiting room," the receptionist said.

A little boy on the floor was playing with a broken truck, his mom sitting close by reading a magazine. He began to make revving noises, and then drove the truck into the leg of the chair his mom was sitting on.

"Can you please stop that, Ethan. It bothers Mommy."

Ethan gave her chair a final smack. Then he pointed the truck at Charlie.

"Ch-ch-ch-ch-ch," he said, imitating a machine gun.

Charlie cocked his head to one side. "Why are you shooting at me? I'm innocent."

"No. You're a bad guy — and I'm the good guy." He fired a few more rounds.

"Doesn't matter. I have an invisible force field," Charlie said. He pretended he could knock his hand against it.

"My bullets have go-through-invisibility-force=field powers," Ethan said.

"But I also have an anti-go-through-bullets chest protector," Charlie said.

"Yeah. I got super-duper mega pointy bullets that totally kick your chest thingy."

"So what. I have an eyeball laser gun and I'm firing at you right now."

Ethan shrugged that off. "Big deal. I got laser-stopping rubber powers and your laser bounces off me and goes back and kills you."

Charlie threw his hands up. "This dude is tough."

Ethan pointed his truck at Pudge. "You want some?"

"Now, now, sweetie. Be nice," his mom said, flipping a page in her magazine.

"You can shoot, but it won't matter since I have mega-bega-lega magnet hands and I can catch your bullets and throw them back," Pudge said.

"Uh-uh," Ethan said fiercely. "I got melting powers in my ears that make your hands drippy and the bullets go through them."

"The kid is good," Pudge said to Charlie. "We better combine our powers. Commence combo crushing action."

They held out their fists and shook them. Ethan ducked behind the broken car.

A lady interrupted their game. "Mr. Joyce. Mr. Moretti. I'm Sarah Martins."

They lowered their fists. Charlie wanted to die.

"Hi . . . sorry . . . hi. I'm Charlie and this is Pudge."

"Please come to my office."

"I won," Ethan declared as they got up to follow her.

Charlie laughed in spite of himself. "You did. Awesome job." He held out a fist and Ethan gave it a punch. Pudge did the same.

"I like that kid. Shows a competitive spirit," Charlie said to Pudge.

"There's no quit in the E-Man," Pudge said.

Sarah held the door open. "Have a seat in here," she said, "and tell me how I can help. I assume this is a school fundraiser."

"Not exactly," Charlie said. "We're here about the Rainbow Café. My mom is Donna Joyce. She owns it."

"Does your mother know you're here?" Her voice had a slightly suspicious tone.

"Not exactly. But she wouldn't mind." Charlie figured he should get right to it. "Did you hear about the fire at the café, by any chance?"

"I was made aware of it."

"Right now the insurance company won't cover the damages. It's a legal thing, and my mom's seeing a lawyer."

"I am not quite sure why we're discussing your mother's business," she said, with a decided edge.

"I know there's a payment due to the bank soon, to this bank. It will be tough for my mom with the café closed."

"I cannot discuss matters relating to an account without the client present. What is it you're asking?"

"She needs an extension," Charlie said bluntly.

"Look. As I said, I cannot discuss this matter with anyone but your mother," she said. "I understand your concern, but this is between your mother and the bank."

"We have a plan to fix the café," Pudge said.

"Are you her son, too?" she asked.

"No. A friend. We only need a little more time, and the café will be up and running and you'll get your money."

She looked at her computer, tapping away. Charlie had a feeling she was reading her emails.

"Boys, I don't want to sound rude, and I wish you luck in fixing the café, but it really isn't the bank's concern. So if that's it, I really have to get back to work," she said.

"But we've organized a crew," Charlie said. "And we have a way to get materials for cheap, practically for free."

She looked up from the screen. "Good luck with the project. But . . ." She pointed to the door. "I really am very busy."

Pudge got up. Charlie remained rooted in the chair. She wasn't listening.

"We have to fix the café. Otherwise my mom has to

leave Terrence Falls for another job, and we just got here, and . . . and . . . is it really such a big deal to give her another few weeks to pay? The bank has lots of money."

Her eyes softened for a moment — but only for a moment. "I'm sorry to hear that. Hopefully things will work out."

She picked up the phone and began punching in a number.

Charlie stared at her. Pudge shook his shoulder. "Let's go. We got stuff to do. C'mon," Pudge said very quietly.

"Terry, I got your email and I wanted to follow up . . . " she said into the phone.

Charlie pushed back on the chair and the legs made a scratching sound. She gave him a look. Charlie ignored her and walked out. He had been holding his breath without even knowing it, and he had to take a couple of deep breaths.

"That was pleasant," Pudge said, closing the door behind him.

"I wonder if she'd melt if we threw water on her," Charlie said.

Ethan was looking out the window of an adjacent office. He fired his truck at them as they walked by. As angry as he was feeling, Charlie could not help but laugh, and he fired back with his fingers. Pudge pretended to lob a grenade. Once outside, they dropped their boards and pushed off. They did not speak for several minutes.

"Okay. So the bank's not on side," Charlie said. "What would Ethan do? Would he quit? Would he give up?"

"No chance," Pudge said. "That dude ain't never quit nothing in his life. He'd just use his anti-quit injection formula."

"That's what we need — a good dose of Ethan's formula."

Pudge pretended to inject him with a needle.

"So what if we don't have an extension? We don't need one. If we get the Rainbow up and running in two or three weeks, that should give my mom a fighting chance to pay the bank — don't you think?"

"Ethan's my new hero," Pudge said.

"What does surrender even mean?" Charlie said.

"Never heard of it."

"It's not even an English word."

They turned the corner.

"We have our work cut out for us, though," Charlie said.

"I got my 'Get the Work Done' energizer spray," Pudge said, and he mimed spraying himself.

"Give me a squirt."

Pudge sprayed him.

"Sergeant, let's go to the Rainbow and assess things," Charlie said, pushing off a few times to gain speed.

"I'm with you, Major."

Charlie knew he was, along with the other guys, and for all their joking around, Charlie knew Ethan had the right attitude. Charlie had let his mom down — and Danny — and his friends. He'd let them all down.

Okay. Charlie Joyce had messed up. Big time.

But Charlie Joyce was going to make it right.

15

STRONG START

A roar went up from the crowd.

"Sounds like they're finally playing again," Pudge said.

"I'll check it out," Charlie said.

A section of the glass had come loose, and the staff had taken forever to put it back in place. He felt like he had been waiting for hours, and there was still ten minutes left in the third period. Nick and Scott were standing at the corner watching the game. Charlie joined them.

"Does Char-Char need his skates tightened?" Scott said.

Nick put his hands on his hips. "Did someone forget to go pee-pees again?"

"I can't sit anymore. Besides, I'm too stoked about the café," Charlie said. "Are you guys still okay to help after the game?"

"Should I answer this time or you?" Scott said.

"I'll take it. You answered the last fourteen times," Nick said.

"You're right. I'm being totally lame," Charlie said. "It's torture enough to wait to play; it's worse to wait until it's over so we can start working. I've gotta make this right for mom . . ."

"Remind me how many times he's mentioned that," Scott said.

"That'll be eighteen since we got here," Nick said.

"I'll shut up now," Charlie said.

A forward in a red sweater took the outlet pass from his defenceman and chipped it off the wall and out into the neutral zone.

"Good. I would like the opportunity to express myself without being interrupted," Scott said. "Now tell me, Nicholas,"

"Yes, Scott."

"Can you show up after the game to fix the Rainbow Café?"

"Finally, someone asking me an intelligent question. What do you think, Charles?"

"I think I'll watch the game five to ten metres away from you guys," Charlie said.

"Why are you avoiding the question?" Scott said. "What are you hiding, Joyce? What's your game? We're onto you."

"Scott, I won't be insulted like this. What do you say to a hot chocolate and a hot dog that has been sitting on the warmer for over three years?" Nick said.

"I say that's the most brilliant idea you've ever had; actually, it's the only idea you've ever had. Lead on, Sir Nick."

The two jokesters headed to the stands. Charlie chuckled to himself and rested his elbows on the railings of the boards. The boys looked to be in minor peewee, and they were pretty good. Hard to imagine he was that small only three years ago. Neither team could sustain much pressure. A defenceman on the black team was free-wheeling in his end looking for an opening. He faked a pass across ice to his defence partner and hit his hard-charging centre up the middle, who in turn shovelled it on ahead to his left winger. A sweet move to the outside and he gained the blue line and banked it off the wall deep into the red team's territory.

Charlie pounded the glass to show his appreciation. That was an impressive display of skill. The Rebels could learn a thing or two from these little dudes. They certainly never quit skating — lots of Rule Two. His thoughts turned to the rebuilding plan. Sometimes it seemed a crazy idea — and other times totally doable. His buds and he had pulled off lots of things people thought were whacked. Maybe this would be another. That cheered him up. He turned to go back to the dressing room.

His good mood vanished. A bunch of guys were milling outside a dressing room. A few were passing a tennis ball between them with their sticks. A couple were half dressed in their shin pads and hockey pants. He recognized them instantly in their distinctive black uniforms. They were playing after the Rebels.

"Has Chuckles learned not to take cheap shots when someone isn't looking?" Jake said.

Charlie reminded himself of his new rule. He was not going to lose his cool. "I'm not sure," he said. "Maybe."

"Wow. Listen to smarty pants," Thomas said.

"Chuckles has become a comedian," Jake said. "Didn't you hear that he was a funny guy?"

"I did not know that, Mr. Wilkenson," Liam said. "Tell us more."

The other Wildcats stopped passing the ball and crowded around to listen in.

"It's not much of a story. A stupid boy and a smelly girl get together and live happily ever after," Jake said. "It's a beautiful love story if you can stand the stench."

Charlie gritted his teeth.

No fighting. No fighting. No fighting.

"Be nice. Chuckles cries easy," Liam said.

"See ya, boys," Charlie said, and he walked to the Rebels' dressing room.

* * *

Charlie's nerves kicked in the second he entered the room, which was weird since he had felt fine until then. After a minute of sitting quietly getting dressed, he realized it wasn't just him — everyone was tense and feeling awkward. They were lacking in confidence after the drubbing by the Snow Birds. And after his pathetic game, he was in no position to give a pep talk. All he could do was play great and prove to them he was someone the Rebels could count on. His game had to do the talking, not his mouth.

"How much time is left?" Pudge asked him.

"Would you believe I forgot to look?"

"I'd be more surprised if you knew."

On cue, as always, Dalton came in with the information. "There are five minutes left in the game. Coach will come in to talk to you guys. In fact, he's coming down the hall right now." Dalton opened the door, and Hilton walked in.

"Thanks, Dalton," he said.

"Did you see the list of materials Dalton put together for the café?" Charlie said quietly to Pudge. "That dude is organized."

"What about the timetable?" Pudge whispered.

"He is awesome," Charlie whispered back. "We'll fix the café in no time."

"The Tigers have won two games in a row," Hilton said. "I saw some of their second win. They love to chip and chase. Their defencemen especially love long passes from the hash marks to wingers hovering near the red line, so watch for that. This is a good forechecking team. That means our forwards have to get back in good time to set up and give the D a solid target, and I want puck possession over wild passes. If you have to dump it out to relieve the pressure, that's fine. But I'd rather see controlled passes to linemates moving to open spaces. Quick feet will kill them. We break down their forecheck and get the puck out of our zone with pace, we can use our speed to win this game."

"Hard on every puck," Spencer said. "Last game we lost the battles behind both nets. That can't happen again."

"We can't get down on each other," Brandon said. "Let's keep the intensity level high — all game."

"And no dumb penalties," Will said.

"Quick shifts, too," Nazem said. "We can't get tired out there. Up and down and off."

Charlie sensed that some of the other guys — and he hated to say it but it was the old Rebels — were waiting for him to jump in. He was their captain, and he was usually the guy that ended a pep talk. Something inside him held him back, however.

"Give me Spencer and Philip on D to start," Hilton said.

The two defencemen punched gloves.

"And I want Charlie out there with Pudge and Dylan."

The room went quiet. Charlie noticed Brandon and Nazem looking at each other. Charlie kept his eyes fixed on the door; and for the first time since the playoffs last season he forgot his ritual with Pudge to be the last ones out the door. As soon as Dalton told them the Zamboni was off he leapt up and practically ran out on the ice. On his second lap Pudge came up beside him.

"You looked like you were being chased by a swarm of bees," Pudge said.

"Sorry," Charlie said. He felt bad now about breaking their tradition. "I'm too stoked for this baby. I took off before I knew what I was doing. Hope it won't be bad luck."

Pudge tapped his shin pads. "I'm guessing a super-stoked Charlie Joyce is just what this team needs." With that he skated away.

Charlie kept to himself the entire warm-up, and he did not even bother taking a shot. He just wanted the game to start. As soon as the clock ticked down to ten minutes, which signified the start of the game, he raced to the red line for the faceoff. The referee was laughing when he came over.

"At least someone is ready," he said. "I guess you're tired of waiting in the dressing room."

All Charlie could do was nod. He did not want to get distracted. With a reverse grip he bent his knees slightly and leaned forward, carefully to distribute his weight evenly across his blades. Hilton had warned him about being too eager and getting up on his toes, which put him off balance and also made it harder to move laterally. The whistle blew and the referee held the puck up over his head, turning first to Andrew and then to the Tigers goalie. The Tigers centre put his stick down. The referee held the puck over the dot.

Their sticks clashed, only Charlie was a fraction faster and the puck went spinning back to Spencer. He sent the puck to Philip. Charlie recognized the play from their practice — the neutral zone counterattack. Charlie faked right and curled hard to his left. Philip took two strides forward and saucered the puck onto his backhand. He took it without missing a step and bore down on the defence. Pudge was gunning it hard down the wall, Dylan on the opposite side. The right defence-man looked undecided. Charlie figured he was the guy to exploit. He waited until Pudge was half a step from the blue line and rifled a sharp pass, careful not to lead him too much.

Pudge blew past the surprised defender and carved toward the net, the goalie coming out to challenge. The left defenceman came across, his stick held low to the ice to prevent a pass across the slot to Dylan. Pudge held onto the puck a moment longer and then fed Charlie in the high slot. Charlie one-timed it to Dylan. The defenceman threw himself on the ice to block his path to the net. All he did was take himself out of the play. Dylan flicked the puck over his legs to Charlie. He considered passing to Pudge, when the goalie dropped to the ice. The top of the net was totally exposed. He took a final step and fired a wrister to the blocker side. Pudge threw up his arms. Dylan wrapped an arm around his shoulders. Barely ten seconds into the game and they had scored.

"Not a bad start," Dylan said.

"Let's focus on the finish," Charlie said.

Pudge gave them each a fist punch. "On to the next goal, dudes. This is nothing."

Charlie liked their attitude. All business. Put the quick goal behind them and work hard, that was the way. Spencer and Philip came over.

"That almost looked like the play Hilton drew at practice," Spencer said, giving Charlie's pads a tap.

"Good puck movement," Charlie said. "Total respect for Rule Four." He gave each defenceman a cuff on the helmet.

They took their places for the faceoff. Charlie won the draw again, this time back to Philip. The Tigers centre pressed forward. Charlie curled into the open seam, and Philip again saucered a neat pass as he broke free. This time Charlie sent it to Dylan as he cut across the middle, and the right winger took it over the blue line on a slant, both defencemen backpedalling frantically. Pudge had followed him in, and Dylan sent a gentle pass between the right defender's outstretched stick and his right foot. Pudge took it on his forehand, and, grinding his left skate into the ice, made the corner and kept going hard to the net.

The left defencemen came over again. Pudge did not slow down. About four metres from the crease to the goalie's right, the two players collided. It was colossal — both players fell, while the puck squirted free near Pudge's hip. Charlie could not believe his luck. He sneaked in, collected the puck, faked a forehand wrist shot to force the goalie to commit to the short side, and then calmly swung it across to his backhand and stuffed it inside the post on the glove side.

He looked up at the clock. Twenty-two seconds. Unbelievable. Two of the easiest goals he had ever scored — and two of the sweetest. All five Rebels met him in front of the net, and the happy players formed a scrum.

"Rebels are playing tough," Spencer said. "I'm liking the dark side."

"Pudge would not be denied," Charlie said. He gave his buddy a tap on the helmet.

"I'll be the battering ram; you be the finisher," Pudge said.

"We got time for two more goals this shift," Spencer said. "Let's hustle for the faceoff." He laughed and began skating backward to their blue line.

Charlie cruised back more slowly this time, to savour the moment. He had wanted to start the game strong. This was over the top. It showed the difference between playing with focus and being distracted.

A somewhat shell-shocked Tigers group set up for the draw. Their coach had called a time out. Charlie could see him talking to his players, pointing at his whiteboard and drawing furiously.

Good luck to him, Charlie thought. The Rebels own this game.

16

. . . TUMBLING DOWN

The game against the Tigers had ended in a massive 7–1 Rebels victory. Charlie's line dominated and between them they scored six of the goals, with Charlie getting the hat trick midway through the third period on a breakaway pass from Spencer at the Tigers blue line. Charlie put his foot up on a chair, his chest nearly bursting with pride, watching his friends organize themselves. They had all answered the call, every one of them. The Rainbow Café would be back in business — pronto.

"I told them my contractor, Matt Danko, needed a garbage bin delivered, and no back talk," Scott was telling the others. "Dalton is obviously learning I'm his go-to guy."

"This Matt Danko must be awesome," Nick said.

"He is. He can do anything," Scott said. "I heard he has x-ray vision."

"I'd like to meet him some day," Matt said. He wasn't laughing, though. "There is one thing you should know. We're going to have to pay for that bin."

"How much is it?" Pudge said to Scott.

"That might've been a good question to ask," Scott said.

"I'll cover it," Charlie said hurriedly. But he was worried. He maybe had two hundred and fifty dollars saved up in his long board fund.

"So what's the plan?" Zachary said.

"Pudge and I took the liberty of drafting a work schedule," Dalton said. He turned his laptop toward them.

"Oh, no. Total disaster," Scott exclaimed.

"What's wrong?" Dalton said.

"You don't have me as the boss. It's . . . impossible."

Dalton looked bewildered.

"You can be boss as long as no one has to listen to you," Nick said.

"That's what I meant," Scott said.

Dalton looked over to Charlie.

"It took me a while to learn, but the best strategy is to ignore them," Charlie said. "Anyway, it looks like today is cleanup. I assume we're loading all the garbage into the bin."

"We have to take down the sections of wall that were charred or damaged by the smoke or burned by the fire," Dalton said. "We might be able to sand away some of the discoloured sections, which would save time. Some of the ceiling tiles can be washed, but as you can see a number of them must be replaced. A few have even fallen down. Probably got wet when the firemen came in with their hoses. And it would look better if we replaced the discoloured tiles, although that is not critical. We'll keep a look out for some when we're salvaging materials; there could be problems with matching up the tiles, however. Unfortunately, some of the dishes will have to be replaced as well. We have some work to do in the dining area, so we should pile the furniture to the side to protect it. I have also taken the liberty of calling a city inspector to tell us whether the electrical system is still intact."

"And don't forget the hood company to figure out how the fire system is supposed to work," Pudge said.

"Excellent reminder," Dalton said. "I apologize for that oversight."

Pudge opened his knapsack and began tossing work gloves to everyone. "My dad's gift to the cause," he said.

Charlie could have kicked himself. He should have thought of that.

"I did some quick research and learned that it really is advisable to wear masks to reduce the intake of dust and soot," Dalton said. He pulled out a bunch of masks and handed them out.

The gloves and masks went right on. Dalton closed his laptop. For a moment no one spoke, until Charlie soon twigged that the guys were waiting for him. "I don't think this is the time for heavy speeches — and I'm sure no one wants to see Scott cry," he said.

"That's not necessarily true," Nick said.

"I think it's stating the obvious to say that when the Rainbow Café reopens there will be some serious eating awaiting you guys — and thanks for this. I owe ya."

"Yes you do, Joyce," Scott said. He pulled his mask over his mouth and held his hands up in the air. "Now, where's the patient?"

Dalton pointed at two sections of the wall. "Those have to come down, and we must remove that section of ceiling also." He walked over to the stove. "I'm also concerned about the wood strapping here."

"The what?" Scott said.

"Strapping is another name for wood that you nail into the outer walls in four-foot intervals to form sections. You stuff insulation into each section and then nail the drywall into the strapping. Strapping is also referred to in the construction industry as studs," Dalton explained, as only he could.

"Nick, now do you understand?" Scott said. Nick nodded. "Please don't ask any more silly questions. You're really annoying today."

Dalton kept going as if Scott and Nick had not said anything. He's learning, Charlie thought.

"A lot of the strapping around the range was burnt, in some places quite severely. I think we should replace it. Some of the insulation has also been singed, and over there you can see how it has even melted. That will have to be replaced also. Remind me to ask Matt's father how to go about it."

Charlie pulled his mask down. "I'm in the mood to destroy a wall," he said. "Who's with me?"

Matt held up his crowbar. "Commence the attack."

"It is time," Scott said, in a super low voice.

Matt pounded the wall with the rounded end of the crowbar in several places. A fine mist of white dust fluttered in the air. "Would you like to do the honours?" he said to Charlie.

Charlie slid the thin end of his crowbar into a hole and pulled back. A piece of drywall broke off and fell to the floor by his feet. It was a good feeling, and he let himself enjoy the satisfaction of seeing the section of drywall torn out. Matt and Pudge joined in, and soon they had most of it down. It was hard work, and Charlie's arms were aching, but he was also totally stoked. How many guys had friends like this? He could hardly wait until they were all back on the ice together. But first things first, he reminded himself, pulling off another hunk of drywall and tossing it over to the ever-growing pile.

* * *

Three wearying hours later, they had made a ton of progress. But what a mess! Taking down the walls had turned out to be a dirty job, with a film of white dust everywhere. The ceiling was even harder, since they had to use a ladder. It was lucky Matt's dad had an extra one. Charlie's spirits lifted when his mom walked in. She was carrying a tray, which could only mean only one thing — food!

"Hey, Mom. You won't believe how much we've done."

She scrunched her nose. "There sure is a lot of . . . dust."

"Yeah. We'll clean it all up, no problem. Taking down the walls was ugly. Before we started we covered what we could with plastic sheets."

"Where did you get the plastic?"

"Pudge brought it."

His mom nodded slowly. "And the bin outside?"

"Scott ordered it."

"Please ask your friends to give me the invoices for the plastic and the bin. I'll pay for them," she said firmly.

A chorus of "Hi, Donna," rang out, followed by one "Hi, Ms Joyce."

"At least I know Pudge is here," she said.

Charlie and his mom had long ago given up telling Pudge to use her first name.

"So . . . what's on the tray?" Scott drawled.

She arched her eyebrows. "What if I told you there are some snacks?"

"May I take a look?" Scott said.

She put the tray on a table and removed the foil.

"Gentlemen, I will do the taste test. Don't thank me. I'm that kind of guy." Scott took a sandwich.

"You might want to wash your hands," his mom said.

"I didn't actually do any work," Scott whispered loudly.

"I was mentioning to Charlie that I'll pay for the bin outside. Are you okay with the one or do you need another?" she asked Dalton.

Dalton looked up from his laptop. "I believe this one should be sufficient. The debris is almost all cleared. I'm reviewing my calculations for the materials we need. I should be done momentarily."

"I'll be done momentarily also," Scott said, chomping on his sandwich. "Did you make any of your famous spiced turkey?"

"If you're lucky you should find a couple," she laughed, and added, "You're a pleasure to feed, Scott."

Scott elbowed Nick. "I told you I was her favourite."

"Our next step is to find the materials for the repairs," Charlie said to his mom. "We'll go hunting tomorrow."

"We have to do it in the morning. We have a practice at three o'clock," Pudge said.

She ran her eyes around the café, seemingly searching for something. Charlie thought she was acting a little odd, like she was sad. She should be getting stoked; the Rainbow Café was coming back!

"How long will you be here?" she asked.

"As long as it takes to clean up," Pudge said. "Few more hours, I guess."

"Matt's dad should be coming over," Charlie said, "to tell us what we need to do next."

"The problem is he's working on a house a couple of hours out of town. He said he'd try to help as much as he could," Matt said.

"I'll give him a call to thank him. It's very generous," she said to Matt. "I've also made a few calls to some contractors and tradespeople I've used in the past. They're all so busy before Christmas, though. Some of them said they'd try to drop by and give us some advice. We'll see, I guess." She ran her hand along the bottom of her purse.

"I'll see you later, then. Take care, boys," she called out, "and thank you all so much. It really is a wonderful thing you're doing, helping us like this."

"No problem," and "No big deal," were the answers.

"Thanks for the food," Scott added.

She laughed. "Don't forget to give me the invoice for the bin — and Pudge, I want to pay for that plastic sheeting. Bye."

Pudge elbowed Charlie. "My dad said I could have it. Tell your mom not to worry."

Charlie was not so worried about that; it was his mom who concerned him. Lately whenever she laughed or joked around it seemed forced, as if it was a big effort. The sandwiches were nice, but better would have been for her to believe in this. Deep down he knew she did not.

17

ONE OUT OF THREE

"I'm finished, Charlie."

"Can you put your plate upstairs, D? I'm rushing around — gotta get going when mom comes home."

"No, probs, big bro."

Charlie winced as he watched Danielle go upstairs with the cutlery sticking out of a cup balanced precariously in the middle of her plate. "Be careful, Danny."

"Yeah, yeah."

He folded the last of the towels and put them into the clothes hamper, and then arched the small of his back until he heard a crack. Strange how tired he was, like the feeling he got when he went shopping with his mom at the mall for clothes. He could play a game of hockey and feel great after, but a couple hours of housework drained his energy, and he still had to empty the dishwasher. He prayed his mom was still up for taking Danielle to drama class. The boys were meeting soon at the café to go look for building materials. It would be very uncool if he was late. He was also getting more worried about his mom. She was always tired — and irritable — just not her normal self. He knew she was totally stressed about her baking business. She was busy, but not enough to make much money, according to her, anyway. He needed to fix the café up, and fast, but it was tough when he was always waiting around for his mom to get back from this place or that. He gripped the hamper with both hands and began to haul it upstairs. With relief he heard the front door close.

"Charlie! Don't tell me you haven't finished yet! Danielle has to go soon." His mom had her eyes closed tightly and she threw her purse on a chair.

"Relax, mom. I've done almost everything on the list. I put this away and make Danny a sandwich and we're good." They had been arguing a lot lately over this stuff. She never gave him a break no matter how much he did. Like now; working like a demon for hours here, and the first thing she did was criticize. He bet she had more stuff for him to do, which meant he would have to cancel on the guys. He asked the question to get it over with.

"Are you going to be able to take Danny to class?" he said.

Her shoulders slumped. "I've been up since three in the morning," she said.

It was like a punch to the stomach. Not unexpected, though. "It's just that I was meeting the guys to get stuff to fix the café . . ."

She pushed a few strands of hair from her face. "Charlie, maybe you should be focusing on getting your homework done instead of —"

"My homework is done," Charlie broke in. He had stayed up late last night to do it, which was probably another reason he was tired. "I think I should focus on the café . . . and maybe you should too, a bit," he added.

"My lawyer told me it will take months to work things out with the insurance company . . . if ever," she responded. "And let's face it, we can't keep going like this. I'm frazzled and you're working so hard and dealing with school and Danielle, not to mention hockey. I had another long talk with Theresa this morning, and . . . I think we will really have to consider Stanville."

That was the one thing he could not consider, not for a second. "Give it some more time, Mom. We'll have the café up and running soon. I promise. We got it all worked out. Just a little longer. It'll be fine."

She bit her lower lip and looked up at the ceiling. Charlie would have given anything to know what she was really thinking. "I hope so, Charlie. I do. Sometimes a situation is . . . too difficult. This might be one of them. Why don't you call your friends and tell them to relax today. It's beautiful out. We won't have too many nice days like this left. I can take Danielle. You meet your friends, and have some fun."

He felt his energy surge back. "Okay, Mom. I'll put this stuff away and fix Danielle's lunch and then take off."

She ruffled his hair. "I can handle the lunch," she said. "I would appreciate you putting the towels away, though. Thanks."

Charlie picked up the hamper. "What time is it, anyway?" he said.

"Almost ten-thirty."

He broke out in a sweat. He should be at the café. "Thanks, Mom. I'll see you back here later." He bounded up the stairs with the hamper in hand.

"Dress warmly," she called after him.

"Gotcha." He began to stuff the towels onto the shelves. Hopefully, the guys would be late too.

* * *

Charlie blew on his hands as he rode on his board along the mostly empty streets. A faint dusting of snow covered the ground and the car windshields were opaque with frost. Once again he had ignored his mom's advice. Then he remembered his construction gloves inside his windbreaker. He slowed down to put them on. Better than nothing, he reasoned — but not by much.

Pudge, Matt and Dalton were in front of the café. He gave a few more pushes and cruised the rest of the way. "Sorry for being late. My mom didn't get home till now and I had to deal with Danny and . . ."

His friends were laughing.

"No one expected you to be on time," Pudge said.

Dalton opened a three-ring binder. "The freecyclers didn't have much for us, unfortunately. I called a few places but nothing developed. On the other hand, we have four potential salvage locations my father sussed out. Two are houses close to here, and also a store. The last is a car dealership on Kingsdale Avenue which is a bit far . . ." He shrugged. "That's what I have for today."

"Awesome," Charlie said. "Let's ride." He shivered and dropped his board down.

They looked at him.

"What?" he said.

"We're just surprised you're not wearing shorts," Matt said.

"Mom told me it was cold, but I'm too cool to listen, apparently."

Dalton pulled a sweatshirt from his knapsack. "My mother was more insistent. Would you like to borrow it? I should be okay in this." He held his arms wide. He wore a down-filled winter coat, a balaclava for under his bike helmet, and ski mitts.

"If you're not using it . . . sure. But tell me if you get cold," Charlie said.

The extra sweatshirt helped, although Charlie could not help but envy his friends in their hats. The three boys rode on the sidewalk. Dalton rode his bike on the street alongside them. In less than ten minutes they arrived at the first house. Through the bay window, Charlie saw a couple of people moving around inside.

"This is crazy, isn't it?" Charlie said to Pudge

"Totally," Pudge said.

Charlie steeled his nerve and knocked on the front door. An older man holding a measuring tape in his hand and a roll of papers under his arm answered it. His eyes narrowed. "Owners aren't here. Not interested in what you're selling." He began to close the door.

"We're not selling anything," Charlie said.

Keeping the door open halfway, the man asked, "What d'ya want, then? We're busy."

"Sorry to bother you. I realize you're busy and all. But we're . . . my friends and me are fixing up my mom's café. It got damaged in a fire, and we're trying to find used materials to fix it up and reopen."

The man opened the door wider. "What exactly do you want?"

Dalton handed Charlie a paper, and he began to read the list. "We need ten sheets of drywall, drywall nails, mud — not sure why we need that?"

"It's for the drywall," the man said, "to cover up the seams between two pieces."

"Right. Thanks. And we need two-by-fours and two-by-eights, which are . . .?"

"That's lumber — I think for your drywall." He opened the door completely.

"Yes. Thanks again. I've got a lot to learn, I guess. Construction is complicated, more than I thought."

He laughed. "It can be."

"And we need insulation, a couple of lights that hang from the ceiling — and paint and tiles if you have any."

The man ran his hand through his hair. "I heard about that café, I think. It was in the papers. Nice lady ran it."

"That's my mom."

"You can get exactly what you need at any building supply store."

"We don't really have the money for new materials," Charlie said. "So we're salvaging."

The man looked uncertain.

"It's a new environmental movement which seeks to recycle materials that would otherwise be thrown out," Dalton explained. "It serves the dual purpose of meeting our financial constraints, and also helping the environment by diverting materials from landfill."

The man stared at Dalton for a second. "Okay. Never heard of that. Used materials, if they have been cut or have nails in them, will be hard to use . . . sounds odd to me. But let me think. Too bad you didn't come last week. We filled eight bins at least. Hmm. Wait a sec." The door closed.

"A week?" Charlie lamented. "Our luck sucks."

"Maybe," Pudge said. "He might have some stuff. He came around there at the end."

The man returned shortly. "You have a vehicle?"

"My dad can come this afternoon with his truck," Matt said.

"Good. I spoke to the owners. I have some old dry-wall for you. I also have some good pieces of drywall, big ones, that you can have. You'll just have to spend more time on the mud."

Charlie's expression must have asked the question because he got an answer without having to say any-thing. "It's easiest to use new pieces of drywall because they're standard sizes. I'm giving you pieces that have been cut, usually because I needed a narrower or shorter piece. You can still use them — but I can't be bothered taking them to another job. I'd throw them out. Now that I think of it, I can give you some mud and drywall nails — and you'll need a couple of rolls of tape, which I can donate."

"Tape for what?" Charlie said.

"Are you doing the work?"

"We are," Charlie said.

"Hmm. Well, the tape is for the drywall. First you tape the seams, and then you put the mud over the tape to cover it up."

"So that's how it works," Charlie enthused. "Awe-some. Thanks."

"Happy to help. Your truck should come before five o'clock. I'll be gone by then."

They said thanks and goodbye, and headed to the second site in very good spirits.

"We should have the materials nailed by today, and we can start the repairs tomorrow morning," Charlie said gleefully over his shoulder to his friends trailing behind.

"Make a right up here," Pudge yelled.

Charlie carved hard, leaning to his right, and for a moment thought he might eat some pavement. But he pulled it off, and turned around to boast to his buds. "See how I pretended to almost fall."

"You gotta stay alive or there's no point to all this," Pudge said.

"There's some logic to that," Charlie said.

They arrived in no time. This house was much bigger, which in Charlie's mind meant more materials. He headed straight for the front door and knocked loudly. Again, a man opened the door; he too carried a tape measure and clutched some rolled-up papers. Must be a construction thing, Charlie figured.

"Hi. My name's Charlie Joyce. Me and my buds here are looking for materials to fix up the Rainbow Café. It got damaged in a fire and we're trying to repair it. We were hoping you could help out with some lumber, insulation or any building materials you don't need or will be throwing out. We have a truck that can . . ."

"We got nothing," the man said. He shut the door.

The four boys stared at it.

"That went well," Matt said.

"Definitely not a former customer," Pudge said.

"Maybe I spoke too fast," Charlie said. "Should I ask again and explain it better?"

"I suggest we proceed to the third site," Dalton

said. "My sense is he would be less than receptive to us asking again."

Charlie turned away. "I think you're probably right," he said.

A less confident group continued onto the third site; and they left it feeling downright nervous. Charlie had barely introduced himself before the door closed in his face. Charlie continued to joke around with his friends as they headed to the final site, trying to block out what was obvious to everyone. This was the last good lead, and after that . . .?

No materials.

That meant no Rainbow Café.

It was that simple.

18

UNBURIED TREASURE

They arrived at the car dealership in a pack. A few trucks were parked in front, along with a front-end loader and a small bulldozer. At the far end of the parking lot stood stacks of paving stones and, next to them, white bags on a skid wrapped tightly in plastic and rolls of thick black paper. The building itself seemed deserted.

"They might have left early," Matt said.

"All we have is some drywall," Charlie worried. "We'll never get this done." He peered through a large window, one of many that stretched across the entire front of the showroom. It was dark inside and hard to see. "I think we got ourselves a dead end, boys," he said.

"Gosh darn it," Dalton said.

The rest of them exchanged glances, then burst out laughing.

"Sorry for the strong language," Dalton said sincerely.

"No worries," Matt said. "It is . . . um . . . a bit of a negative development."

"I concur."

"Hold on, fellow scavengers," Pudge said, his face pressed up against the window. "I see signs of life."

They all looked back in.

"Definitely humanoid. We should investigate," Matt said.

"I've got an idea," Charlie said. He went to the front doors and began to knock.

"Brilliant," Pudge said.

A figure emerged from the darkness and came to the doors.

Charlie grinned. "It worked."

"What's up, boys?" the man said, stepping out.

He seemed friendly enough. Charlie summoned his courage and told him what they wanted.

"That's a big undertaking; you don't have a contractor?" he said, when Charlie had finished explaining the situation.

"Matt is sort of the unofficial contractor," Charlie said.

"My dad's a carpenter," Matt said, "and I help him sometimes. Dad said he'd try to help us, but he's tied up with another job right now."

"I guess we're winging it," Charlie said.

"I can't really give you any new stuff that we don't use up. The owner is a bit of a fanatic about that and he makes sure that any extras are used for the next job. Let's just say he doesn't throw money around."

"What are you building?" Charlie said.

"This is going to be a new Dunn's Sportsmart. He already has one downtown, so I don't know why he needs another one here, but the guy's got tons of money and he must know what he's doing. I could ask the owner, Tom Dunn, if you'd like. You never know. He might let you have something. What's your name?"

Charlie didn't know whether to laugh or cry. Tom Dunn was practically the last guy on earth that would help them. He had kicked Charlie off the Hawks last year, which turned out to be a favour, of course, because that's why he and Pudge had started up the Rebels.

"Thanks, but I don't want to bother him," Charlie said.

"I've worked with freecyclers before on other projects — and with other owners — and I know you guys also can find useful stuff from materials that are going to be thrown out," he said.

"We would be more than happy to pick through your refuse if that is at all possible," Dalton said.

He laughed. "Come on in, boys." As they followed him to the main showroom he flicked on the lights and held out his arm. "Help yourselves."

Charlie had never seen such a beautiful sight. And to think a few days ago he would have thought this was junk. Pieces of lumber were piled up at the far side of the room, all shapes and sizes, and next to that, light fixtures, and on the other side of the room, ceiling tiles; they might not match perfectly with those in the Rainbow but they were the same colour and close enough. This had to be everything they needed, and more.

"It all has to be cleared out in three days. Take whatever you need. It's garbage to me," the man said.

Charlie was too overwhelmed to speak. Until this moment, he'd been trying to ignore reality and convince himself they could get this done. Now he was beginning to believe it.

"We're going to need everyone for this," Charlie said to Pudge.

He had the phone to his ear. "Already on it . . . Yo, Scott. We hit the jackpot . . ."

Charlie crossed his arms, and wandered around for a closer look. While everything they needed might be here, most of it was twisted and jumbled together. It would take time to pick out what was useable. He put his gloves on.

"Thanks a million for this," he said to the man. "I really appreciate it, more than I could ever say."

The man waved him off. "Like I said, it's garbage. This stuff costs a fortune to throw in the landfill, and it spares me the trouble of loading it in a truck. Every piece of lumber you take saves me money, so go crazy, boys. Just be careful. There are nails sticking out everywhere and you don't have steel-soled boots." His phone rang. "Excuse me. I need to take this." He walked away.

Charlie went over to the lumber pile. He took hold of a piece and tugged. It held firm. He pulled a little harder, then harder still, and then put a foot on the pile for leverage and put all his weight behind it. It didn't budge. They were wedged in tightly by the pieces on top. This was not going to be easy.

"Are you ready to go hunting for treasure, matey?" Pudge said to him, pulling his gloves on.

"I thought I was Major?"

"The pirate theme seemed more fitting in this case."

"I'm ready, Redbeard," Charlie said.

They began to pull pieces of wood off the top of the pile.

19

TEAM EFFORT

Charlie let out a groan as he leaned down to fish out his gloves from his hockey bag. His arms were beyond sore and he could barely open his hands. He and Pudge had gone nuts on that pile of wood. Scott, Nick and Zachary had caught a lift from Nick's mom and had joined them, and together they had collected a ton of great stuff, although there was still more to do. Dalton figured they'd need another day. The man offered to drive the materials to the café if they loaded it into his truck, which was awesome because Matt's dad had called to say he could pick up the drywall at the first house, but he was too busy tomorrow to help.

The boys had been so into their work that they almost forgot about practice. If it had not been for Dalton they probably would have. It was fun though, hanging out together.

"Don't worry about us," Scott had called out to them as they left. "Who cares about guys with broken arms and legs — we're expendable!"

Pudge called ahead to his dad to bring his equipment to the rink, and fortunately, Charlie had left his equipment at Pudge's house after the last game. His dad was happy to get Matt's stuff too. So with nothing else to worry about, and the three "expendables" working on the pile, they formed a long board–bike convoy and snaked their way to the arena. Charlie rolled his neck and stretched his legs to try to get rid of the tiredness in his body. For probably the first time in his life he really did not feel like playing hockey.

He checked out his gloves. The tape holding the thumb together on his right glove was slipping off again, and the rip on the side of the other glove was getting worse. He hunted around his bag for tape. As he fixed his glove he looked around the room. Most of the guys were leaning against the wall staring into space. No one was talking.

Dalton opened the door. "Zamboni's off," he said.

Matt sidled up next to Charlie and Pudge. "I've been dying to play for weeks and it finally happens and all I want to do is take a nap," he said.

"It'll be awesome to see ol' number ten on the ice again," Charlie said. "Once Zachary comes back we'll have three lines."

"And all our problems will be solved," Brandon said as he walked by them and reached for the dressing room door.

"I just meant that . . ." Charlie began.

"I'm joking, dude," Brandon said. He was not smiling, however.

Charlie had no idea how to take it. "Well, at least Matt can spell you and me at centre. I could use a shift off once in a while."

Brandon looked over at the three of them. "That makes some sense. I'll give you that." He paused and seemed on the verge of saying something, and then just as quickly seemed to change his mind and he left.

Charlie followed his teammates onto the ice, deep in thought. Was that a breakthrough moment with Brandon, or was he being sarcastic? Had the great game against the Tigers united them, or had it merely papered over the divisions in the team? He knew there was still something missing, something that the entire team could rally around. As he dug his blades into the ice and picked up speed behind the net, he racked his brain to think of what that could be.

Hilton blasted his whistle and called them over to centre.

"I've noticed a few teams are playing a 1–3–1, which I have strong feelings about, as you know. It slows the game to a snail's pace, it's boring, and it's against the spirit of the game. Still, we have to be prepared. It's not all that different to a traditional trap. There are several ways to beat it. Here's one, and the good thing is it fits with the Rebels philosophy.

"As with the trap, the key to beating the 1–3–1 is puck movement, hard skating and good decision-making. The moment you see them set up three across the neutral zone and there's no pressure on the puck, run this play. D1 carries the puck straight at the lone forechecker to force him to commit. Then he hits D2 who should be going full steam. At the same time, all three forwards take off, the right winger going deep, the left winger cutting across ice and the centre to the area in front of the lone defender.

"If each defender takes a forward, then D2 carries the puck over centre and dumps it in. Once he crosses our blue line you can expect the forwards to collapse, so you have to make that quick pass. First option is always to the winger on your side, in this case the right winger. The centre is option two, with the left winger being your option of last resort. Remember, short passes to players moving is what we want. You stand around and wait for the pass, the 1–3–1 will smother you before you get started."

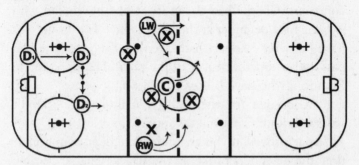

He lowered the whiteboard. "Lots to take in at once. Why don't we do something radical and try it; and with Matt back we have eight forwards, so we'll go with three sets of wingers, and Charlie and Brandon alternating centres. Speaking of which, let's hear it for Matt's return."

Charlie noticed the new Rebels were a bit reserved — but they still joined in to cheer Matt.

"Good to be back," Matt said when the cheers died down. "Thanks."

"Give me Charlie with Jonathon and Pudge as the attacking line, with Spencer and Philip on D," Hilton said. "Defending will be Brandon, Nazem and Will, with the twins playing back. Robert, I want you on the right side covering Pudge. Christopher, you're the rover at the back. Brandon will be the forechecker. The rest of you file onto the bench and pay attention. Watching others mess up is a good way to learn."

Hilton blew his whistle and passed the puck to Philip. Brandon took his place at the blue line and held his stick out to cut off the inside lane. Philip went straight at him. Two metres away he cross-iced a pass to Spencer, but it was a bit ahead of him and he couldn't control it. Charlie had cut in front of Christopher who was the lone defender at the far blue line. He should not have bothered. Robert had taken advantage of the bad pass and stripped Spencer of the puck. He flipped it to Brandon, who gave it back to Hilton.

"Score one for the 1–3–1," Hilton said. "Don't worry, though. This will take some time."

That proved to be an understatement. Time after time the defenders broke up the attack. Charlie became discouraged. The 1–3–1 was impenetrable. Hilton gave the puck to Philip, who once again pressed forward toward Brandon. This time his pass to Spencer was on the money. Charlie curled into the space in front of Christopher. Robert covered Pudge cutting across. Nazem converged to stop Spencer at the red line. Will moved to his left to guard against a pass to Jonathon. Christopher drifted to the left also.

Charlie suddenly got it. The passing lane would be open to him because Christopher had vacated that spot. "Yo, Spencer," he called.

Spencer saw it too. Charlie broke with the pass and crossed the blue line just on side. He was in alone. Martin readied himself for the breakaway. Charlie faked a snap shot at the hash marks, threw in a stutter step to force the goalie to commit to his butterfly, and then lifted a backhand inside the post on the glove side. It was a sweet goal, but Charlie would never celebrate at a practice and show his goalie up. Instead, he turned back laughing and slapped Martin's pads.

"That always works in practice. In a game I can't lift it more than an inch off the ice," he said.

"I wanted to give you some confidence," Martin said, hopping up on his skates. "Give me your A-move next time."

Charlie came closer. "Don't tell the guys, but I don't have one."

Martin gave his shin pads a tap with his paddle and whispered, "They already know."

Charlie laughed harder this time and gave Martin's pads a final whack before heading back to centre.

They lined up again, with wingers and defence pairings switching it up, and slowly Charlie felt things get sharper. The defencemen began to make better choices. The forwards hesitated less often. Charlie was relieved to see Matt fitting in so easily. He was a strong skater and played only one way — full out. Charlie saw Spencer talking to Matt after those two connected on a play. Perhaps his instinct about his new teammates was right; they were coming around.

Finally, Hilton blew his whistle to end the practice. "An impressive effort, gentlemen," he said. "I have a good feeling about our next game against the Hornets. It looks like we're starting to put things together. So far it's been a few shifts here, a period there — I want you thinking about putting together a solid three periods," Hilton said.

"We put together three periods, and then three games," Charlie said. "Time for us to put together our playoff run."

"Amen to that," Matt said.

"Give me a quick three laps and then off the ice," Hilton commanded.

Charlie was determined to set the pace, and he flew off the mark down the side wall and then, leaning hard on his inside leg, carved behind the net and again back up the wall. He heard heavy breathing behind him: it was Spencer. The big defenceman could wheel with the best of them, and Charlie was not surprised he was next in line. But Charlie was not going to let him win that easily. A quick glance over his shoulder suggested Spencer was going to try and beat him when they got to the back wall. Charlie stayed out wide as he crossed the blue line and only when he got to the hash marks did he dart to his left, almost brushing the goalpost with his shoulder as he powered around the net.

"Not bad, Joyce," Spencer said, maybe a metre behind him. "I had a feeling you'd cheat."

Charlie turned his head slightly. "You can still enjoy watching my back for one more lap," Charlie said.

Spencer laughed. "I think it's time we traded spots."

Brandon, Will and Jonathon were obviously unaware that this was a race, and they were taking their time. Charlie and Spencer bore down on them. At the red line, Charlie swung to his right just as Will began to swing his arms around as he told a story. Charlie had to duck and jump to the side, and he could do little to stop Spencer from cutting in between Brandon and Jonathon and taking the lead.

"Now who's cheating?" Charlie called out, laughing.

Spencer pumped his fist in the air. Charlie gave it his all but Spencer had too much of a lead, and in half a lap there was no way he could catch him. Spencer stopped at the door with a flourish, sending a massive shower of snow into the air. Charlie did the same, but with the advantage of being able to cover his teammate with snow, rather than the boards.

"I'm very disappointed in you," Charlie said. "Not sure you're mature enough to apologize right away, but take your time and try to get the words right."

Spencer nodded, as if in serious contemplation. "That's a good idea. I think I'll wait a couple of years."

Charlie gave him a forearm to the chest, and opened the door. "Leave me alone. I need to cry this out."

He hopped off the ice.

"Guys seemed a bit more stoked for the practice today," Charlie said cautiously, interested in hearing what Spencer thought. The new Rebels looked up to Spencer, and if Charlie could get him on side, the rest would follow; at least that's what he hoped.

"I admit I'm getting a bit stoked about Hilton's system. I'm understanding what he means, maybe not all the time, but once in a while. It's amazing the difference when you're moving your feet, getting in position, and looking at the entire ice."

Dalton held the dressing room door open. "Good practice, gentlemen," he said.

"If our manager's happy, then it must have been good," Spencer said. Then he laughed to show he was joking.

"He obviously didn't see your disgraceful performance," Charlie said.

Dalton's face fell. "Oh dear. What happened? Is there a problem?"

Was there a more sincere guy in the world, Charlie wondered? He gave Dalton's shoulder a clip with his glove as he walked past. "I'm only kidding, Dalton. He beat me in a race, and now he's so arrogant he's impossible to be around."

"Not true," Spencer said, flopping on the bench. "My problem is I'm so awesome it's painful for others to be in my presence."

Dalton looked helplessly at Charlie and then said in a whisper, "He's joking too, right?"

"You're definitely catching on," Charlie said.

"I have noticed that I sometimes take things too seriously and fail to appreciate the levity of the situation," Dalton said.

"Dude, don't change — you wouldn't want to end up like him," Spencer said, pointing at Charlie. He held out a fist and Dalton gave it a tentative punch.

The rest of the guys piled in, and the dressing room became a lively place.

Will was still holding court with Jonathon and Brandon. Pudge and Matt were talking about the lines for the Hornets game, and Dylan was finding a song he wanted Nazem to hear. Only Christopher and Robert were quiet. Dalton came over to Charlie.

"Zachary just called from the dealership," he said. "They have separated the materials we can use, and apparently they will be delivered to the café in less than an hour. We might need to hurry and get over there."

"What café are you talking about?" Spencer said. "Is that your mom's place?"

"Is your mom fixing it up?" Jonathon asked.

"What's Zachary doing?" Brandon said.

Charlie looked pointedly at Dalton, who reddened stepped back toward the door. Maybe he had not told Dalton specifically to keep things quiet, but Charlie thought that was obvious. The entire situation was embarrassing to him. He did not want everyone on the team to know his business, and he absolutely did not want them to know he might have to leave the team. The Rebels had enough to deal with this season already.

He had to give them an answer, however. "It's nothing," Charlie said. "We're just cleaning things up for my mom. Zachary's helping, since he can't practise."

"Who else is helping?" Jonathon said.

The room was quiet again. "My mom's been working hard starting up a new business, baking for people, events and stuff like weddings . . . and stuff . . . and she's had no time to deal with the fire. I asked some of the guys to help me."

"What are you guys doing there?" Robert asked.

"Just cleaning up . . . fixing things a bit."

"I assume Scott and Nick are helping . . . with Zachary," Spencer said.

"I . . . um . . . think so," Charlie said. "Well, obviously I know . . . they are." Charlie wished they would stop grilling him about this. Why did they care so much, anyway?

"And Pudge," Jonathon said.

"And Matt," Brandon said.

His friends nodded. The new Rebels, especially

Spencer, looked disappointed. Will shook his head a few times and tossed his gloves slowly into his bag. Nazem took a few deep breaths. Even more disturbing were the reactions of the original Rebels, like the twins, and Jonathon and Dylan. They looked downright mad — and he had to assume they were mad at him.

Then it dawned on him. They had the right to be mad. He had done it again, but this time even worse, ignoring not only the new Rebels but also many of his teammates from last year. In his effort to keep his problems a secret, he had caused more problems for the Rebels. Charlie lowered his eyes to the floor.

"I didn't want to bother you guys with all this stuff; maybe that was dumb. Truth is, me and Pudge, Matt, Zachary, Scott and Nick . . . and Dalton . . . are trying to fix up my mom's café, replacing some walls and ceiling tiles, repairing the range, lots of stuff." He leaned back against the wall and looked up. All his teammates had stopped undressing and were waiting for him to continue. He hesitated for a second, but that was all.

Because now he really understood what Rule Five was all about.

"My mom's business isn't going so great; well, it's going, but apparently it will take more time; and the bank wants money from her and the landlord and . . . well . . . to complicate things my mom's been offered a job at a restaurant, which is great; what's not great is it's in Stanville. We'll have to move. And . . . I guess that's it. We're trying to repair the damage from the fire so she can reopen and make some money in time. It's a long shot — a total long shot, but we figured it was worth a try."

"But wouldn't the insurance pay for that?" Dylan asked.

That was a question he could have done without. But he had gone this far. "The fact is the fire was my fault. I left the range on the night we played the Wildcats, and that's why the insurance company won't pay us. My mom's got a lawyer, but it'll take months to figure out, apparently."

"And what are Zachary, Nick and Scott doing again?" Brandon said.

"Dalton had the idea of salvaging the building supplies we need," Charlie said, "which basically means we take stuff people are throwing out or don't need from other construction sites and reuse it."

"Let me get this straight," Spencer said. "You caused the fire by leaving the stove on, and you dudes think you can fix it yourselves."

"I suppose," Charlie said.

"And you're getting the materials from the garbage."

"Essentially."

"And if you don't pull it off, you have to move to Stanville."

Charlie nodded.

"When do you need us?" Spencer said matter-of-factly.

Charlie leaned against the wall, staring back at him.

"If you want, right after practice," Dalton said, jumping in. "We have a shipment of materials arriving soon."

Spencer glanced quickly at Brandon, and then over at Will and Nazem. Each nodded ever so slightly. Jonathon flashed a thumbs-up, as did Dylan and Martin. Andrew had leaned over to untie his pads. He looked up and nodded also.

The twins looked at each other. "We're in," Robert said.

"Sounds good to me," Spencer said.

Charlie was overwhelmed.

"We can all meet at the Rainbow Café in about an hour," Pudge said. "This is awesome of you guys. We'll get it done in half the time now."

"I will revise the schedule in light of the additional manpower," Dalton said.

Charlie still did not trust himself to speak. He wished his mom could have seen what had just happened. That would have convinced her. A picture of the café came to mind.

Look out Rainbow. You're about to get a Rebels makeover.

20

NEW RECRUITS

Charlie held the arena door for his mom.

"Good luck, Charlie," she said, taking a sip of coffee. "Who are you playing again?"

"The Hornets," he said and, lowering his voice, added, "They're not the best team in the world . . . so we should win this one."

"I thought it was one shift at a time," she said.

"Are you becoming a hockey insider on me?"

She arched her eyebrows. "I've watched you play a few thousand games, so I've picked up some lingo along the way. Anyway, you should get going. Your game starts in less than an hour."

Charlie searched for the Rebels on the dressing room listings — and felt his heart fall to his feet. In a panic he looked at the teams on the ice and then the scoreboard. "I don't get it," he said. "That game is almost over, and there's two games now before ours. Did I . . ."

"Oh, Charlie. Did you get the time wrong?"

"I thought Dalton said 8:10 . . ."

"You told me 7:10."

He flushed. "You may have a point there."

But his mom did not laugh. "It's been a long day and you made me rush to get here . . ."

For a second he thought she was actually going to cry. She had been like this for a while now, always irritable and emotional. He did not know what made him do it, but he went over and gave her a hug.

"Sorry, Mom," he said softly. "Another one of my dumb moves."

She hugged him back. "Yes it was — but I forgive you because I know your brain is still too small to remember game times."

"Thanks for understanding," he said, and they both laughed. "You don't have to stay. It'll be two hours before we start. Go home and I'll catch a lift with one of the guys."

"Are you sure?"

"No worries. You can watch game number three thousand and one next week — when we play the Wildcats. And, like, how big is that game?"

"Um . . . Totally awesome?"

Charlie shook his head slowly. "You'd probably want to go with 'Massive' or 'Huge.'"

"I guess I'm still learning. I'm a bit too tired to be 'Cool Mom' right now anyway. I think I will go home and rest up for the Wildcats. Gotta beat the Wildcats!"

"Now *that's* a 'Cool Mom' thing to say."

She gave him a kiss and turned to leave.

With an hour to kill, a snack would be nice. "Hey, Mom," he called out. She turned. Her face was lined with worry. "I'll . . . uh . . . see you later, at home."

"Okay, dear. Have a good game."

He walked to the stands slowly. With the way things

were he did not need to spend her money on junk from the snack bar, that's for sure. He carried his bag up the stairs and laid his sticks across it. The game was almost over. By the size of the players he judged them to be atoms. A forward for the blue team took a huge back-swing and tried a slapshot, missing the puck completely and falling on his butt. He could remember doing the same thing a bunch of times when he was a kid. His dad kept telling him not to worry about slapshots, but he would not listen, and his dad had been prouder than anyone when he finally learned to raise the puck. He had to laugh.

"Be nice to the little guy. He's cute."

His old friends the butterflies kicked in. Julia was sitting across the aisle a few seats in, feet on the back of the chair in front of her.

"What are you doing here . . .?" he said.

She peered at him from under her hat. "I had a practice before this game. Becca and Alex are coming to watch your game, and I figured I'd hang with them too. I didn't feel like going home and coming back, so I decided to stay. I've texted them — they'll be here soon."

"Since when did they become such diehard Rebels supporters?"

"Is Brandon playing?" she asked.

"Yeah. Why?"

"We went out, the girls and I, with him and Spencer and Nazem to a movie — and then for ice cream — last week. Brandon invited us. It was no big deal, but that's why Alex is coming." She took off her hat and ran a hand through her hair. "I believe Alex may have a slight

crush on him. Don't tell anyone or she'll kill me —
although I think she's told everyone anyway. You know
Alex."

Charlie's chest tightened. "That's cool. I mean,
they're good guys. Good players too, especially Spencer.
Awesome skater with the puck, sees the entire ice. I can
see why you like him."

Arms crossed and leaning back in her seat, Julia took
a deep breath. Charlie thought she looked a little
flushed, like she had a fever.

"Are you feeling okay?" he asked.

"I'm fine, Charlie." The buzzer sounded to end the
game. The blue team had won and the players raced
from their bench to mob their goalie. "Are you going
to be antisocial the whole time?" she said.

He looked around. "Antisocial? Why? No. I mean. . .
What do you mean?"

She sighed and patted the seat next to her. Charlie
grinned awkwardly and moved across the aisle.

"You must be pretty stoked for this one. Why so
early?" she said.

"More stupid than stoked. I got the time wrong."

She threw her head back and laughed. "Of course
you did."

"That'll be our little secret, right?"

"I won't tell anyone . . . except Scott and Nick and
Alex and Mr. Hilton . . . and I should probably update
my Facebook status and share it with all my friends.

"Okay. But it can't go beyond that."

The gates opened and the Zamboni came out. The
conversation suddenly lagged, and Charlie felt at a loss
for words.

Julia retied her ponytail and then put her hands in her lap. In a soft voice she said, "Spencer told me about the café . . . and about Stanville."

If she knew, then everyone must know, which kind of bothered him. It was personal stuff. Julia was different, of course. She was a friend. But he did not want all the kids at school bugging him about it.

"Is it true? Do you really think you might have to leave Terrence Falls? You've only been here a year . . ."

He quickly told her about his mom's situation. " . . . But we've been going hard at it at the café," he continued. "The entire team is helping, which is awesome. Spencer's been helping too . . ."

She furrowed her brow. "Since the entire team is there I assumed that meant Spencer too."

She did not sound happy. He was forever saying the wrong thing. But what had he said this time? She obviously liked Spencer, and he thought she would want to know Spencer had stepped up, that was all. "I just meant —"

She cut him off. "So when do you boys get working again?"

"Tomorrow after school."

"Count us in. We want bragging rights also."

"Who's we?"

"Me, Becca and Alex. I want in on saving your butt — again."

"Again?"

"Saved your life on the bus; saved you in that dodge ball game with Jake; saved you from making a fool of yourself in front of student council when we were fundraising. Shall I continue?"

"That should do it for now." They *had* been through a lot together, come to think of it. "It's hard work —" he began.

"And since we're girls . . ."

"I didn't mean that!"

She sighed. "You really don't get my zany sense of humour, do you?"

He would have to agree with that. "Meet us at the café at four o'clock, and if you promise to be nice to me for the rest of this game, I'll organize a pair of work gloves for each of you."

She put a hand on his arm. "When I heard that you were leaving Terrence Falls," she said, "I almost . . ."

"Go, Rebels, go! Go, Rebels, go! Go, Rebels, go!"

Scott crossed over to where they were sitting. Nick was coming down the other aisle with Rebecca and Alexandra. Julia crossed her arms and put her feet back up on the chair. Nick slipped his cane under the seats.

"When did you start sporting one of those?" Alexandra said to Nick.

"I find a cane better suits my lifestyle," Nick said.

"Those are two things I never connected with you," Scott said, "a life, and style."

The players for the next game came out and began racing around the ice. Alexandra checked her phone. She giggled.

"Brandon's so funny. Did I show you this?" She held her phone out for Julia to look at the screen. "You didn't answer my text about the party," she added. "Brandon, Nazem and Spencer are going."

Charlie kept his eyes glued to the ice. He noticed

Scott was focused on tying his shoelaces, and Nick was fiddling with his cane.

"I know. Sorry. It's just that I might be busy," Julia said.

"Come on, Jules. You gotta. Becca's already committed. A guy at their school rented out a hall and there's a band and food and everything. Tickets are cheap, too. Please. Pretty please."

"Okay. Fine. It's probably okay."

As hard as he tried to ignore the growing knot in his stomach, the thought of Julia going to a party with Spencer bothered him more than he wanted to admit. Which was dumb because Julia was just a friend and she could go to a party with whoever she wanted. Scott was not looking too happy either, but then it was common knowledge that Scott had a thing for Rebecca.

The referee's whistle sounded and the players began to line up for the faceoff.

"So Brandon tells me you guys had a good game last week," Alex continued. "He doesn't know where Matt will play since he and Charlie are the centres . . . "

"I like Matt up the middle," Scott said. "He gives us more speed and power, so Charlie doesn't have to carry the attack all the time."

"Excuse me?" Alexandra said.

Julia caught Charlie's eye and smiled. Alexandra certainly was not going to allow her Brandon to be dissed by the likes of Scott.

Charlie tried to smooth things over. "I think he means that a third centre gives us more options. I, for one, like having a breather. Playing every other shift is tough."

"Come on, Joyce," Scott said. "Brandon ain't in Matt's league. We all know that. I think we should shift Brandon to the wing."

"Brandon can play, but we're talking Matt," Nick added.

"Sorry to interrupt your little lovefest," Alexandra bristled, "but you guys are full of yourselves, and trust me, some of the players don't like it."

"Alex!" Julia said.

"It's true. You're always on about how things will be okay when Matt gets back, and Zachary, and Nick and Scott. How do you think that makes the other guys feel?"

The three boys didn't answer. Finally, Scott said, "I didn't exactly mean it that way."

"Yes, you did," she said. "You may not have meant to put them down intentionally, but you have to admit you don't think the Rebels have a chance without Scott, Nick, Zachary and Matt playing."

Other than what he thought of Spencer's skill on the ice, Charlie had to admit she was right. But there was more to it. Just like when they started to fix the café, he and his buds had only been thinking about themselves, their little group. None of them had given any thought to the rest of their teammates. Now he realized the same was true about the team. Charlie always thought of his closest friends as being the core, the most important players. But a team needs different types of players, and his crew were not the only guys that could play. Spencer, Nazem and Brandon were solid — more than solid; and they along with the other new Rebels were the same guys killing themselves to save the Rainbow. While things might not have been going as fast as he would like, they had cleaned up, organized the materials, cleared away the damaged drywall and ceiling tiles and chipped away some of the discoloured floor tiles.

"That's not the way it is," Scott said. "And how did you get the inside info anyway? It's Brandon, I bet."

She flushed. "That's not the point."

"But he's the leak, isn't he?" Scott pressed. "I figured him for that."

"For what?" Alexandra said.

Scott shrugged her off. "Not your team, not your worry."

"Whatever."

This could be bad, Charlie thought, and just when things were looking up. If Brandon and Alexandra were friends, and this got back to him, Charlie would be back to square one in uniting the Rebels. The bottom line was that Alexandra was right, regardless of how she found out. But he did not want to pick sides against Scott. Anyway, he had a feeling the thing Scott cared about most was Rebecca going to that party, not whether Matt or Brandon played centre.

"Alexandra, maybe you have a bit of a point," Charlie began tentatively. "We do tend to talk about things getting better when the guys hurt in the accident come back, and let's face it, the team will get better. At the same time, the new guys have stepped up and done awesome. We have more points this year than we did last year at this time. I hate to say it, but Alexandra's probably right about us. We've never given the new Rebels a real chance. In fact, why are we still calling them the new Rebels? It's like we're ten-year veterans or some-thing."

Nick picked up his cane and started to tap it on the floor. "I can't believe I'm about to say this, but I guess you're right. But do we have to actually agree with Alex?"

"Is that so bad?" Alexandra said.

Scott squirmed in his seat and cleared his throat. "Best thing would be for Alex to apologize for making us realize we're jerks, and just get it over with," Scott said.

"Is this how really immature boys apologize?" Alex-andra said.

Charlie could tell she was trying not to laugh.

"Not entirely," Scott said. "We also do a fist bump."

"Come on. That's so . . . juvenile." But she reached out and tapped her fist with his.

"And there's more," Scott said. He held his forearm out. Alexandra bumped it with hers.

"Not quite done," Scott said. "This is the hard part. You gotta quack like a duck and do a dance. It looks like this."

Scott began quacking away, squatting low with his butt stuck way out and turning around in a tight circle.

"You need to do it too or the apology doesn't work," Nick whispered loudly.

By this point the girls were laughing too hard to answer. "Please stop," Julia barely managed to spit out, "People will think we know you."

Scott sat down. "Not *our* fault. She demanded an apology," he said, pointing to Alexandra.

"You should be apologizing for what I just saw," Alexandra said. "Go buy us some hot chocolate."

"Alex, you're relentless," Julia said.

"Shush, you. Now shoo and hurry up, boys," Alexandra said.

"She makes sense to me," Rebecca said.

"It's usually my policy never to agree with girls under any circumstances, but a hot beverage and a snack might be just the thing we need in this situation," Scott said.

"It's my policy never to agree with Scott, but he's probably right," Nick said. All of a sudden Nick looked up at the scoreboard, and then at Charlie. "How come you're not getting dressed?" he said.

"I got the time wrong and came early," he said. "I thought the game was at 7:10."

"It is," Scott said.

Charlie shook his head. "It says 9:10 where they list the dressing rooms."

"Which is why we told the guy in the pro shop that they mixed the games up and he changed it," Nick said.

Charlie did not know whether to laugh or cry — and if no one had been there, maybe it would have been the latter. "Excuse me while Hilton yells at me for being late again."

He left to the sound of their laughter. It *was* funny, but he was not in the mood to laugh at himself. He was in the mood for things to go his way, for him to get a break. He was tired of pedalling up a mountain all the time.

It would be nice to coast downhill once in a while.

21

A STEP BACK

Brandon lost the draw and the puck spun to the Hornets' left defenceman. Ryan forechecked, and the puck carrier banked it sharply off the boards to his left winger. He clearly thought he had some space, for he took a few steps with his head down to gain speed. Robert stepped in and made him wish he had been more careful.

Scott cheered from the stands. "Massive hit."

"Awesome, Robert!" Nick called out.

Brandon and the Hornets centre battled for the loose puck, which rested against the boards about two metres past the red line in the Rebels side of the ice.

"It's yours, Brandon," Charlie said.

The Hornets player slipped the puck between Brandon's skates and legged it free, curling into the middle of the ice.

Christopher had swung over to challenge. The centre wisely chipped the puck in and gave chase. Jonathon came back off his wing to retrieve the puck.

"Take the left boards," Charlie muttered. Under Hilton's new system, Brandon should cover for Jonathon. Instead, he circled in the slot for a pass. That put him and Dylan on the same side, along with Chris and Robert.

Pudge saw it too. "Might have a slight case of the bunchies," he said.

With all five Rebels on one side and under pressure from the oncoming centre, Jonathon flung the puck behind the net and around the far boards. Brandon broke off too late to get it and it squirted past him to the Hornets right defenceman. Jonathon stepped up to cover the other point, and Dylan as the right winger hustled across to the other side. Christopher and Robert settled into their positions down low. The only problem was that everyone had forgotten about the Hornets centre behind the net. He sneaked in behind Robert to Martin's right, a metre out from the crease. At the last second Charlie saw it. He stood up.

"Behind you," he screamed.

The defenceman rifled a beautiful diagonal pass to the centre, who turned his stick sideways and deflected it into the open side. Martin had barely moved.

"Running around in our own end," Hilton said. "You guys know better. We lost two battles for the puck, didn't play hard in front of our net, and the result was a goal against. Hockey's a simple game, even when you're playing badly. Now put that behind you and focus."

He folded his arms across his chest and stared stonily toward centre. Charlie lowered his head and tapped the top of the boards with the shaft of his stick. He was burning to get out there, but Hilton had started Brandon, this time with Jonathon and Dylan on the flanks, and he was not going to shift things up just yet. Made sense, too. Better to give the boys on the ice a chance to redeem themselves.

The puck dropped and this time Brandon knocked it to the right boards. Dylan flicked it past the winger and charged forward.

"Hold on," Charlie said to Pudge. "This looks promising."

The left defenceman went straight at him, determined to hold the blue line. Dylan surprised everyone by faking an outside move, then sliding the puck between the defenceman's skates to set up a two-on-one. The other defender cut over and held his stick to cut off the pass. Dylan glanced to his left. Brandon had slowed at the high slot, his stick on the ice, clearly looking for a pass. Jonathon had a slight step on their right winger, but it would be hard for him to do more than rush the net. A metre inside the circle, Dylan swept his stick toward Brandon. The defenceman bit. Dylan immediately pulled the puck back to his forehand. The Hornets' defenceman refused to give up, however. He scrambled to his left, forcing Dylan to make a quick decision: shoot or pass. He chose to shoot.

Charlie got to his feet. The far side was wide open. The goalie had overplayed it —

"Don't do that!" Charlie said. He could not help himself. Dylan had missed the net by a metre, and the puck had wrapped around the boards. Jonathon reached for it, and he got the tip of his stick on it, not enough to get control, but enough to slow it down so the Hornets right winger could pick it up easily.

Just like that the Hornets forwards surged out of their zone on a three-on-two.

"Was that supposed to happen?" Pudge said.

"Spencer and Philip will shut it down," Charlie said.

But after a token move inside, the puck carrier busted it wide right. Both defenders were caught flat-footed. Neither had expected such an aggressive and simple move. Martin stayed back in his net, playing for the deke, probably because the puck carrier was coming in so fast. Bad decision, as it turned out. He feigned a backhander, brought it over to his forehand, dipped his left shoulder and roofed a wicked shot under the crossbar.

As painful as it was to watch, Charlie had to admire the goal. "That was a beauty," he said. "No chance for Martin."

He and Pudge got up, assuming Hilton would call for a change. That had been two goals in forty-five seconds. But again Hilton remained with his arms crossed, a slight frown the only indication of his mood. They sat back down.

"Perhaps he wants us to strategize some more," Charlie said.

"Perhaps he wants to lure the Hornets into a false sense of security before we pounce and score ten unanswered goals," Pudge said.

"Two–nothing in less than a minute; we're doing a good job on the first part of the strategy," Charlie said.

Zachary put a hand on their shoulder pads. "Would you boys mind scoring two quickies?"

Philip had the puck behind the Rebels' net. He brought it out the right side. Dylan and Brandon crossed, like they were supposed to, with Jonathon sweeping across the top. The forechecker waved his stick wildly from left to right. Philip looked to pass to

Brandon against the boards, but then hesitated and dropped the puck.

"Get to it," Pudge yelled.

Spencer should have followed up. The puck sat there in the slot. The Hornets centre took it on his forehand and shot in one motion — another goal. Martin stared up at the ceiling. Philip did the same.

"Brutal," Zachary said. He banged the top of the boards with his fist.

"Now that's the really brutal part," Charlie said, pointing to the goal scorer. It was none other than Mike Dunn; a more obnoxious guy Charlie had never met. He was not mean like Jake and his crew, and he was basically harmless — just hard to take most of the time. He definitely liked scoring against the Rebels, and true to form he was windmilling his left arm, his right arm holding his stick high over his head, like he had just scored the overtime winner for the Stanley Cup. He glided toward the Hornets' bench, balancing on his left foot, stick still held high.

Spencer dug the puck out of the net and fired it down the length of the ice. The referee came over and said a few words to him. Spencer simply nodded. Hilton had one foot on the top of the boards. He called Spencer over and leaned down.

"Switch," Hilton said before Charlie could hear what he was going to say to Spencer. Hilton did not take kindly to temper tantrums. He hopped the boards and headed to centre.

"Don't worry about it, guys," he said to Brandon and Dylan as he passed them. "One bad shift. You'll get it back."

They did not respond. What was there to say? Barely a minute gone and it was 3–0. The ref held the puck over his head and then over the dot. Mike crouched for the draw. Charlie had to stop himself from smiling. Mike always did the same thing: reverse grip and pull it back to his right. As the puck fell, Charlie thrust his stick between Mike's skates to tie up his stick. He then spun his butt into Mike's midsection to create space and allow him to shovel the puck with his forehand back to Robert.

The referee's whistle immediately halted play. Charlie quickly counted the Hornets players. He guessed they had too many men. But they had five skaters, just like the Rebels. He looked up at the clock. It was working. "What's the call?" he asked.

The ref looked at him as if he had just asked the dumbest question in the world. "You're in the box for two minutes."

Charlie turned around. "Who?"

"Number eight. In the box," the ref snapped.

A penalty on him! "For what?" he demanded.

The ref skated to the scorer's bench, and he made a chopping motion with his right hand to his left arm.

"Slashing?" Charlie yelled. "I never touched the guy."

"Into the box, number eight," Mike said from behind. Charlie whirled around. Mike flashed a toothy grin. "Learn to play by the rules."

"I never slashed you," Charlie said.

"That's not the point," Mike said. "The referee thinks you did, which is good enough for me."

"Forget him," Pudge said. "Dumb call. We'll kill it."

"Or the Dunnster will snipe his second," Mike chimed.

"You're hard to take, Dunn," Charlie said.

Mike laughed. "I'll give you the puck after I score."

"Now that's actually funny," Charlie said. He tapped Pudge's shin pads and headed to the penalty box.

Hilton sent out Matt and Nazem for the kill, with the twins on D. Charlie felt bad for Pudge having to miss his shift, and doubly bad for putting the Rebels in such a bad spot, even if it was a bogus call. Matt won the draw and Christopher blasted the puck off the boards and down the ice. The Hornets goalie trapped the puck behind the net and left it for his left defence-man, who waited for his teammates to set up. Mike curled in front to the right, and the defenceman fol-lowed him up ice. Matt forced him at the top of the circle and the defenceman lofted a pass up to Mike, who was looking back for the puck the entire time.

Charlie had noticed Robert cheating up from the blue line. He could feel the pain coming. Robert low-ered his shoulder and Mike was lifted off his feet and crashed to the ice on his back.

Instantly, the ref's hand went up, and a groan sounded from the Rebels supporters.

"No way," Charlie said, smashing the glass with a glove. "You're still allowed to hit in hockey. Two bad calls in a row."

Scott and Nick were booing in the stands, and the Rebels were on their feet yelling. None of it did any good, of course. The referee tapped his shoulder to indicate charging, and Robert came over to the penalty box. Charlie opened the door for him.

"You're gone, number five. That was a hit to the head," the referee said.

"That was perfectly legal," Charlie said, leaning onto the ice. "He never came close to touching his head."

The ref's eyes blazed. "One more word out of you, number eight, and you'll be outta here too. Now shut that door."

Charlie had to use every ounce of self-control not to diss him back. Refs were hard to take sometimes. They had all the power and they never listened, even when they were wrong. He knew it was a tough job, but still. Robert stared at the ref, and was about to say something, when he simply shook his head and left for the door. Boos cascaded down from the stands.

Pudge came over to serve Robert's five-minute penalty.

"A two-man advantage for five minutes and thirty-eight seconds," Charlie said, as his buddy sat down. "How much worse can this get?"

The sat glumly and watched the Hornets pass the puck around the Rebels' zone. About thirty seconds later Charlie found out that things could get a lot worse, as the Hornets left defenceman sneaked in the back door to convert on a sharp cross-ice pass that nicked Martin's blocker and bounced into the bottom corner of the net.

"It's been a slice," Charlie said. "Catch you back at the ranch."

This was supposed to be the start of the playoff run. He did not know what was worse, to be losing 4–0 in the first period or to have to listen to Mike Dunn bragging about it at school. Brandon was setting up at centre, so Charlie went to the bench. Hilton remained in his arms-across-the-chest pose, his frown now much, much more pronounced.

22

BITTER SWEET

Crack!

Matt tossed the broken tile into the garbage can.

"This is impossible," Matt cried, throwing his gloves on the floor. "It can't be done. The guy at the hardware store said this would cut any tile. We've busted six already." He slid the tile cutter across the floor and threw his gloves at it.

Julia took her gloves off too and, shoulders slumped, shook her head from side to side. "I've read and re-read those instructions ten times. We're doing everything right. Maybe we got a defective model."

Charlie came over. A bunch of floor tiles in the kitchen had changed colour because of the splattered oil. They had agonized over whether to replace them; but when they found tiles at the car dealership that were very close in colour they decided to do it. Charlie thought the luck in finding the tiles was a sign that they should go for it, and he figured it would be a nice thing for his mom to see. The only problem was the new tiles were bigger. They had laughed when the first tile they cut had broken. It did not seem so funny now.

"This could be a job for your dad," Julia said to Matt. "Is he going to be able to come?"

Matt looked pained. "He promised to try, but I wouldn't hold my breath. The owner is crazed about the job getting done before Christmas, and my dad's been working fourteen-hour days."

This was their fourth straight day working after school. Things took so long, though. Things Charlie thought would take ten minutes would still not be finished two hours later, and half the time whatever it was looked so bad it had to be redone. The cleaning up had gone so well, but it had been all downhill from there, and Charlie could tell the boys were getting discouraged. It had taken them a day to just chisel the broken and scorched tiles out, and they had made a mess of the job on top of that. He was thinking they should have left the tiles alone.

"Speaking of impossible, I can't put on the drywall mud without leaving a massive line," Zachary said. He had white muck all over him. "The YouTube video made it look like a joke — but the joke's totally on me, dudes."

He was right. The walls looked like garbage. In fact, the café looked like garbage.

Dalton turned around from the stove. "I am really getting cross with this appliance. I cannot understand why the timer will not function. I've checked it ten times. Now I'm worried the used motherboard is defective."

"What's a new one cost?" Charlie asked, bracing himself.

Dalton's face fell. "It would be prohibitive. Maybe seven hundred dollars, or more like a thousand."

"That's crazy," Charlie said.

"Not as crazy as the ceiling tiles," Pudge said. His face was beet red and covered in sweat. "They are held up by these metal tracks with slots. The new tiles are a tiny big bigger than the old ones and we can't get them into the slots without damaging the tracks. We've wasted an hour on one tile. And don't suggest cutting them. We butchered a few tiles already."

"Have we made any progress today?" Charlie said in a loud voice.

"Scott learned to hold a hammer," Nick said.

His joke fell flat. Charlie struggled to keep calm. "Okay. Not a big deal. We need a new plan. Maybe we should all focus on one thing instead of everyone dividing into little groups. Maybe . . ."

Spencer came down from the ladder. Tapping his hand with a screwdriver he said, "Charlie, I understand this is seriously important for you. It's just that . . . Well, I'm not sure the plan is the problem."

"I'm open to any ideas," Charlie said.

"That's just it — I don't have any," Spencer said.

"Not sure that will work," Charlie said.

Spencer waved his hand at the walls. "Look around, Charlie, Nothing is working. We don't have the skills."

"And I'm gonna fail my English test if I don't study," Philip said.

"I think we're too tired," Charlie said. "The guys who need to study or go to sleep should take off. That's cool. Get stoked for tomorrow and . . ."

"We have a game tomorrow," Dalton said. "Against the Wildcats."

"Great. I really feel like getting stuffed by Jake," Scott said.

"Because we suck so bad? I'm really getting tired of being told how great the Rebels will be when you guys are healthy. I know you can play, it's not that, but come on — it's not like we're not trying. " Spencer said.

. Scott turned pale and he spun the hammer he was holding in his hand. "No one sucks. I meant . . . we're tired . . ." He didn't finish.

"Rule Five, guys," Charlie said. "Let's not get down on ourselves, or each other. Once we nail Hilton's new system, we'll smoke the Wildcats, *and* the Snow Birds for that matter. We're just going through a rough patch." He picked up another tile.

"I'll stay and work a bit more," he continued. "No problem. There are probably too many bodies getting in each other's way. I'll figure out some shifts, too. That way we aren't working all at the same time and guys can get homework done and stuff. I'll email something to Dalton tonight, and you too, Pudge. Look it over and let me know if it makes sense. You guys should take off and rest up."

"It's not that . . ." Spencer said.

Charlie was getting frustrated. "What is it then?" he said.

"We need a professional. We don't know what we're doing. This might've worked if your mom had hired some people," Spencer said.

"It's not her fault she doesn't have the money," Charlie shot back. He felt his blood beginning to boil.

"No one said it was," Pudge said.

"There *is* a bit of a skill gap," Nick said.

Charlie struggled to take it in. He could understand Spencer getting tired of working, and he assumed the other new Rebels were fed up also. To hear Pudge and Nick, his closest friends, side with Spencer — what was going on? He looked around. None of the guys would meet his gaze, including his buds, and they all seemed to be shifting their weight awkwardly from one foot to the other.

Crash!

Charlie spun around. A newly installed ceiling tile had fallen onto the floor, breaking into large pieces. A thin film of dust floated in the air. He felt sick.

"We should call it a night," Zachary said. He looked totally worn out.

"Probably makes sense," Matt said, wiping his hands on his sweatshirt.

"Sorry, Charlie," Jonathon said. "It was a good idea . . . "

All of a sudden he understood. It hit him like a thunderbolt. They were not just going home for the night. They were leaving for good. The new plan was to give up. They didn't have the skills. It was as simple as that. In a flash he accepted what he had suspected but had ignored for the past couple of days. The weirdest part was he did not really feel upset. In fact, he felt calm, even relaxed.

"You guys are right. What can you do? That's life. Leave the tools. I'll deal with it tomorrow. Most of them are Matt's dad's, or my mom bought them. Thanks for the help. I still owe you. You didn't have to do this, none of you. We'll focus on the Wildcats. That's a huge game."

"Can't lose to the Wildcats. It's against the laws of nature," Scott said.

Spencer came over. "This isn't right. There's gotta be something we can do."

Charlie waved him off. "You guys have been awesome. Way above the call. Let's win that game tomorrow."

Spencer held out his fist. "We still good?"

"Definitely."

They bumped fists.

Zachary held out his fist next. "See ya later, dude."

"Cool," Charlie said.

The guys said their goodbyes and began to file out. It was all very low key and almost surreal for Charlie, as if this was just a normal day instead of the end of the Rainbow Café. His mom had been right after all. It had been a big waste of time.

"If you're lonely playing tomorrow you can climb into the stands for a hug," Scott said to him.

"We're here for ya, baby," Nick said.

"I know it," Charlie said. "I'll definitely see you there after the second period."

A horn sounded. Dalton ran out to see who it was. He came right back. "Matt, I believe your father is here."

"Now my dad comes?" Matt said, throwing his hands in the air.

Pudge placed his gloves down on a table. "Catch you later," he said to Charlie, and turned to leave.

Charlie grabbed his sleeve. "It was a good try. Our luck just ran out."

Pudge nodded, and seemed about to say something

when he shrugged, crossed his arms and looked toward the door. Matt was coming back.

"I may as well take my dad's tools now," he said.

"I'll help," Charlie said, and he began to pick up a few tools around him. He reached for a hammer lying on the floor.

"I got that," Julia said.

"Thanks. Cool." He and Julia gathered a bunch more tools and loaded them in the truck. The driver's side window rolled down.

"Hello, Charlie. Sorry I cannot help with café more."

Charlie could see how sorry he was by the look in his eyes. Charlie had a soft spot for Matt's dad ever since he had done some work for his mom when the café first opened.

"No worries. We tried, and I sure learned a ton, mostly that there's a reason people do this for a living." He tapped the bottom of the window frame. "I really appreciate the tools."

"I do anything for Miss Donna," he answered. "I am stuck at job too much. Very sorry. Tell her I am free after Christmas — as much as she need." He gestured to the back seat. "You kids need lift? Jump in."

"I'll call my mom,' Charlie said. "I have some stuff to load up too. But thanks."

"I called my dad already," Julia said. "Thanks."

Charlie tried to catch Pudge's eye, but he looked away and got into the truck. Matt hopped into the front passenger seat, and the truck pulled away. Charlie waved and turned to face Julia. He hoped her dad would come soon. He wanted a little time by himself, to take it all in.

Julia interrupted his thoughts. "I think Pudge was kind of upset," she said.

Pudge had put everything into this. Of course he would be totally bummed out. He would call Pudge tomorrow to make things good again. Pudge sometimes blamed himself for things that were not his fault.

"I guess I'm not too happy either, to be honest," he said. "But I'll get over it. I feel bad for my mom. She loved this place."

"It's awful what happened." Julia rocked up on her toes and with a rueful look said, "Um . . . This is awkward . . . but I should tell you that I didn't actually call my dad to pick me up."

Charlie laughed. "I didn't call my mom either. I wanted to be here a bit longer. I know I have to deal with reality, but I figured it wouldn't hurt to put it off."

She grasped her wrist behind her back. "I should've realized you'd want to be alone. I'll call now. Sorry. That was stupid of me." She pulled out her phone.

He let out a carefree laugh. "Put it away. I'll walk you home. No biggie. It's not that cold. I've spent enough time here."

"Are you sure? I don't mind."

"Seriously. It's cool."

She put her phone in her knapsack, took a deep breath and looked at Charlie with an intense expression. "That would be nice — and I wanted to talk to you, anyway."

"Let me lock up first, and we can talk on the way," he said.

Charlie went back into the café. A few of his mom's tools were still scattered about. The broken tiles were piled in the corner. White dust from the drywall coated the floor. He could only shake his head and chuckle, a bunch of kids making a mess. Just like that it was over, as if it had all been a dream, and now he was back in reality. "It's been nice knowing ya," he said, giving the empty room a salute; and with a lump in his throat he turned off the lights and locked the door.

They crossed the street and headed toward Julia's house.

"So what's up?" Charlie said. He could tell she was nervous about something.

"Ever since the game against the Hornets, I wanted to finish our conversation. I think I might've given you the wrong impression about us going to the movie with Brandon, Nazem and Spencer, and about that party. I only went because Alex begged me — to even out the numbers, if you know what I mean."

Charlie wasn't exactly sure. "I didn't think anything. I mean, you can go, obviously . . . I mean, you can do what you want. It's cool. And I think those guys are cool too, and I'm going to make it right with them, let them know I don't think they're the second-raters on the team."

"The Rebels aside, I wanted you to know that, for me anyway, they're just friends. Nothing more," Julia said.

They continued in silence, and then Charlie said, "I'm sorry if I gave you the wrong impression. I was being lame. I shouldn't have presumed anything was going on — not that it's any of my business. Anyway . . . sorry."

"Charlie Joyce, now you are being lame!" She put a

hand on his arm and they stopped, facing each other. She looked sad. "There is only one boy I want to go to a movie or a party with." Her eyes were a bit misty and she wiped them. "I was trying to work up the courage to ask *you* to come to the party with me, to go together, and then Alexandra came and blabbed about it, and with everyone there it was too weird."

They continued walking, and Charlie didn't know how or when it happened, but by the time they arrived at her house they were holding hands.

"I . . . um . . . probably would've said yes," he said, suddenly.

"About what?"

"The party. It would've been fun."

With a mischievous smile she asked, "Do you remember how we met?"

Of course he did. "At the dodge ball game last year. You tricked Jake into throwing the ball at you instead of me. You caught him out — and then got me out, which was a vicious double-cross, by the way."

"I was only trying to get your attention."

"You did."

She slid her hands to his shoulders and, leaning forward, gave him a kiss. "Goodnight, Charlie."

She waved from her front steps before disappearing inside. Charlie began to dribble a piece of ice along the sidewalk as he walked home. It was really not that warm out. He stuffed his hands in his pockets and picked up the pace. Soon his house came into view. He saw his mom's silhouette in the living room.

With a heavy heart, he opened the door.

23

THE LAST WALTZ

Charlie found he couldn't look at his teammates. Instead he focused on carefully retaping two of the fingers on his right glove. He wasn't sure how to tell them. He had only told Pudge, and Pudge had barely said a word to Charlie since. Charlie inspected his left glove. It was holding in there, so he left it alone. Hilton had gone over the game plan a few minutes before, and had barely started his pep talk when he cut it short and left. Charlie sensed it wasn't going anywhere, and probably he did too.

Something was missing. It was that feeling in the dressing room when you know your team is stoked, that perfect mixture of nerves, confidence and calm — that combination of focus and excitement that takes you to a higher level. He looked around. The Rebels did not believe in themselves. They had taken steps forward as a team, only to fall back again. It was as if their failure at the café had been the last straw.

Charlie gathered his nerve. It would be the last thing he would ever do as captain of the Rebels. He could only hope it worked.

Dalton came in. "Coach Hilton has asked me to let you know that the game has been delayed due to an injury on the ice. The Zamboni is only just now coming out."

He turned to leave.

"Stay here for a sec," Charlie said to him. "I wanted to say something to the team and I want you to hear it too."

Dalton looked surprised. "Is there something I can do?"

"I don't need you for anything, other than to hear this. Bit of an announcement — a new development, I guess. First off, I gotta give you all huge props for the work at the Rainbow. Maybe we didn't pull it off, but it wasn't for lack of effort. It got me thinking last night, though. Better to lose as a team than win as individuals. The first Four Golden Rules of Hockey are all right, but Rule Five is the king. I've said this before, and I wanna say it again, for the last time. This will always be my team. Charlie Joyce will always be a Rebel."

No one responded. The silence hung heavily.

"Is this about the café . . . and your mom?" Zachary said.

Charlie dropped his gloves in his bag. "My mom told me this morning, me and Danielle, who's my sister, by the way, for those who don't know — she's the one ringing the cowbell most of the time. Anyway, my mom doesn't think she can make enough money just selling her baking. She's working insane hours, up at three in the morning and when she's not going to bed early, she's up real late getting stuff done. She said she can't keep going like this —"

"You're leaving, aren't you?" Scott said. His face was white as a sheet.

"Couldn't you stay until after the school year . . . or at least the season?" Nick said.

"She's taken a job in Stanville, in a restaurant. We have to leave after Christmas."

"Christmas is in one week," Dalton said.

"Don't I know it. We'll stay with my mom's friend for a few weeks and then move into another place my mom has found to rent. She wants us there as soon as possible to arrange for things — school . . ." He forced a grin. "I ain't dying, guys — I'm coming back to watch you kick the Snow Birds' collective butt in the finals."

No one laughed.

"My dad said he could help after Christmas," Matt said. "I kinda thought that might save things."

"My mom doesn't want to wait," Charlie said, "and she doesn't think the bank will wait either. She's made up her mind, I guess."

"This is a huge loss for the Rebels," Spencer said. "I know this must be a killer for you and your crew. I feel bad for your mom, and bad that we couldn't get it done for her. Tell her I'm sorry. And I'm not sure the finals is gonna happen without you, dude."

Charlie knew exactly what to say. "That's not true. This is the best team in the league. All we need is confidence. All year it's been excuses: guys are hurt; we're playing a new system; it's just a rough patch. Forget all that. I'm not leaving this team as a loser. This is bigger than me having to move. This is representing. This is stepping up when it hurts inside. It's suck-it-up time. I ain't gonna look back on what might have been with the Rebels. I'm gonna look back at how the Rebels slaughtered the Wildcats one more time."

"A Wildcats butt-kicking does intrigue me . . ." Nick said.

"I'm with Charlie on this," Spencer said.

"True dat," Brandon said.

Charlie could have run through a wall he was so ready to play. "This is the game when we put it all together, boys. We stop *thinking* about Hilton's system and we just *do* it. We totally commit. It's time for Rebels hockey, which means playing a thousand kilometres an hour — and hard. This game is over the minute we step on the ice. Everyone here agree?"

They sure did, and the team chant of "Re-bels! Re-bels! Re-bels!" started up.

Charlie held his hands up to quiet them down. "This is my last game as a Rebel, and my last game wearing this C on my jersey. We're a team — and that means no player is more important than another. We win or lose together, and that includes these two strange dudes who are in the stands every game, Zachary working the door, and each of the guys wearing a uniform in this room.

"We may not be much of a construction crew, but I say we're the best team in the East Metro Hockey League, and after this game, the Wildcats are gonna know it. This is Rebel-time, boys."

Dalton opened the door and did a quick check for time.

"The Zamboni has a final lap and then we're on," he said.

"Hands in," Charlie said, standing up in the middle of the room, and the Rebels solemnly held their gloves out. "That means everyone," he said, and Scott, Nick and Zachary added theirs. "You too, Dalton," Charlie ordered.

"No regrets after this game," he continued. "No wondering what if we'd only pushed harder, fought for that puck a little more, backchecked a little faster. We're Rebels to the core, and we're gonna play like that. Do it, Spencer."

"Uh-uh. Captain leads this cheer."

Charlie took a deep breath. "Rebels on three," he shouted. "One . . . Two . . . Three."

"Rebels!"

Martin and Andrew led them out. As was their tradition, Charlie and Pudge held back.

"Weird to think this is our last game together," Pudge said.

"I still remember the first time Hilton put us on the same line," Charlie said.

"At practice, for the Champions Cup team."

"And you got two goals."

"Because you set me up."

"Maybe we should do that again, for old times' sake — and maybe add a few," Charlie grinned.

They punched gloves.

For the first time since the night at the café when they stopped working Pudge looked Charlie square in the eye. "If it weren't for you, I'd still be that pathetic kid always being bullied by Jake, scared of his own shadow. You're the best friend I've ever had."

"That's never gonna change," Charlie said. He gave Pudge's shin pads two whacks, then two more. Pudge did the same to him. Together they walked out. Pudge hopped onto the ice and began to race across the blue line. Charlie paused a moment. The Rebels supporters were sitting together behind their bench. Scott and Nick were leading the cheers. Next to them he spotted Julia, Rebecca and Alexandra. Brent, the team sponsor, was there too. Charlie's mom and Danielle were standing, Danielle clanging her cowbell like crazy over her head. He felt the weight of responsibility, to the Rebels, to his family, to the people cheering, to his coach, and it felt darn good. He was going to enjoy this game for all it was worth.

He stepped onto the ice and pushed off. Spencer snapped a pass to him. Charlie cradled the puck with the tip of his blade, and then hit Dylan streaking down the middle to take a shot on Martin.

* * *

The puck ricocheted off the boards and spun on its side, stopping at the Rebels' blue line. Liam and Robert ignored the puck entirely and lowered their shoulders simultaneously for a hit. They both bounced backward, stunned by the force of the check. Charlie and Jake were the nearest players to the puck and they bore down, arriving at the same time. Charlie was smaller than Jake, but he felt as if he could lift half a ton with one arm. Jake tried to create space by extending his elbow. Charlie dug his edges in, bent his knees and drove a shoulder into Jake's ribcage.

"Loser," Jake grunted.

"Get your own puck," Charlie replied, as he flicked it back to Robert.

Robert pushed the puck up ice, and when Roscoe cut over he saucered a pass over his stick onto the blade of the breaking Pudge.

"Enjoy this," Liam said with a sneer. The shaft of his stick buried itself into Charlie's side.

"This too," Jake said, delivering a vicious cross-check just above the elbow.

Charlie absorbed the blows and took off down the ice. He would not be goaded into a fight in this game — no chance. As much as those cheap shots had hurt, Charlie had only one purpose. Jake and Liam were behind the play, and if Charlie got there in time he could support the rush.

Pudge looked over his shoulder and then veered to the right sharply, to the centre of the neutral zone, leaving the puck about three metres from the blue line. Matt was there to gather it up, taking it hard toward the left wall. All the while, the Wildcats right defenceman watched on warily. Once Matt crossed the blue line, Pudge made a beeline for the slot, and Robert, suddenly as offensively minded as Spencer, drifted to the left to give Matt an outlet.

All this time Charlie was killing himself to catch up. Matt slowed at the top of the circle, took a step toward the defenceman, and gave it to Robert. Without a second's hesitation, Matt drove around the defender, who had to peel off to cover him, which gave Robert more space to move closer to the net. Roscoe cut across the top of the Wildcats' zone to stop him. Robert waited until he was less than two metres away and flicked the puck between his legs. The puck landed flat and settled in the slot, two metres before the hash marks.

Charlie collected the puck in full flight. He could sense Jake and Liam behind him. Matt fought for position near the goalie's right, and Pudge battled to his left. He did not have much time. Best to shoot, he figured, and he was about to pull the trigger when the defenceman covering Pudge surprised him by throwing himself on the ice to block the shot. Charlie jumped and swung the puck wide to his forehand. The puck barely slipped past the sprawling player's skates, but Charlie was not as lucky and the tips of his blades caught the player's shin pads. He felt himself become airborne, heading for a painful crash landing.

Somehow the puck was still on his stick, however. He considered a shot until a familiar voice changed his mind.

"Char. Over."

Charlie lowered his left shoulder and hooked the puck to Pudge at the side of the crease. The rest was a blur. He landed on his shoulder, his helmet also taking a good knock, and spun over once before sliding into Matt and the other Wildcats defenceman. A pair of gloves thudded into his back and his face was pressed onto the ice. His chin struck with a fair bit of force so that he might have been seriously hurt if he had not been wearing a cage.

"Stay down, loser."

He felt another sharp blow to his head.

"Play is over, boys," the referee said.

Jake gave him another none-too-gentle push at the back of his head and got off. Charlie was on his feet in an instant. Enraged, he took a step toward Jake, who was laughing at him, egging him on. Charlie almost threw a punch. At the last moment he relaxed his arms and lowered his gloves. That was not the way he was going to end his last game in a Rebels uniform; Rule

Five would not let him. In that moment, his anger melted away. The Rebels supporters were cheering like mad, and he could hear a cowbell ringing. Pudge had his stick over his head, and so did the twins. They had scored the first goal.

"You got away with another cheap shot, Wilkenson," Charlie said. "But you also cost your team a goal. Looks like I win again."

Jake did not seem too bothered. "I'll get it back when I feel like it. More important to trash your face."

"Be nice. You know how sensitive he is," Liam said.

Pudge thrust himself so close to Liam that their facemasks were only inches apart. "You don't look so tough up close."

Liam backed away, but his cocky grin wasn't going anywhere. "Pudgikins is cranky — quick, get him a doughnut!"

Pudge laughed him off. "You're a broken record. Same lines for ten years."

Charlie moved over so he and Pudge were shoulder to shoulder. For a few moments it was a staring contest.

The referee stepped in between them. "Are we going to have problems today?" he said. He blasted his whistle and pointed to the centre dot. "I'm happy to give a penalty to anyone who wants to keep mouthing off."

Even Liam kept quiet.

Charlie and his teammates celebrated their goal with a few high-fives as they headed to the bench for a change. Danielle's cowbell continued to clang above the cheering din of the spectators.

"Awesome rush, Robert," Charlie called over to the

defenceman at the other end of the bench. "That was your goal." Robert merely blushed and nodded his head a few times. Charlie tapped Pudge's shin pads. "I still owe you one more."

"No kidding. I'm not letting you off the hook. Only you don't have to kill yourself to do it."

"Small price to pay."

Zachary gave both of them a slap on the back as they settled in. "Heart and skill, dudes. They can't stop that." Leaning closer he added, "and good work not taking a penalty. They'll be after you guys all game."

"Let 'em," Charlie said. "Makes me feel better."

He rooted around the front ledge for a water bottle. His arm, where Jake had cross-checked him, brushed against the butt-end of Jonathon's stick. He winced and almost dropped the bottle.

"I like the flow and intensity level so far," Hilton said to them all. "Only we need to win the war, not the battle. They'll come back at you twice as hard. Are we ready for the challenge?"

Charlie took a big sip. He was hurting, but he couldn't have cared less. He was determined not only to meet the challenge, but to fly over it. "One goal means nothing," he said to his teammates. "We increase the effort level and take the play to them. We crush their spirit and the game is ours. We win this game one shift at a time."

Spencer dove at a loose puck and knocked it free to Philip before sliding sideways into the boards. His partner one-timed it off the wall and out of the Rebels' zone to relieve the pressure. Spencer was very slow getting up, but he did not even look to the bench. A shake of

the head and he was right back in the play.

"Next shift, we have Charlie going out with Jonathon and Dylan," Hilton announced.

Charlie stood and put his foot on the edge of the bench. Nazem had won the puck on the right side and with a nifty inside move had some space to push forward in the neutral zone. Instead of forcing another rush after a hard shift, he got over centre and dumped it in deep. All three Rebels immediately headed to the bench, breathing heavily. They had given it their all.

"Nice shift," Charlie shouted as he flew off the boards and took off to pressure the Wildcats defenceman camped out with the puck behind his net.

24

BACK TO WORK

For the remainder of the first period and then the second, both teams settled into a tense, bitterly fought rhythm, as the Rebels and the Wildcats took turns storming the net, each playing with a desperate intensity. The harder the Wildcats pushed, the harder the Rebels pushed back — a case of an unstoppable force meeting an immovable object.

Charlie took a short pass from Christopher on his backhand and, cutting sharply at the top of the circle, powered out of the Rebels' zone. The Wildcats were changing on the far side of the ice, a bad change too, which gave him some room. Matt had shifted over close to centre, with Pudge camped out by the left wall a couple of metres across centre. In this situation, Charlie was tempted to go it alone and see if he could beat the Wildcats' defence. A turnover at the blue line nursing a one-goal lead was inexcusable, however — and selfish. He gained the red line and reared back as a signal to his linemates to take off. When they were about a metre away from the blue line he lofted a forehand in Pudge's direction.

Pudge had been a monster on the forecheck all

game. Again he beat the right defenceman to the puck, absorbing a big hit in the process and. keeping his feet moving. shovelled it around the back of the net to Matt at the hash marks. Charlie had drifted over to Pudge's side waiting for things to develop, and when he saw the Rebels had control of the puck, he snuck down low. Matt banked it off the wall to him. Charlie pressed his skate against the wall to stop the puck and then kicked it up to this stick. By then Jake, Liam and Roscoe had flooded back to defend, with Liam in the high slot, Roscoe covering Christopher at the left point, and Jake and the right defenceman bearing down on him.

If two guys were on him, Charlie reasoned, a Rebels player had to be open. Pudge took his customary spot in front. Matt drifted into the slot. They were covered. That left Robert wide open at the right point. Charlie considered a pass to him. Again, he decided it was too risky. "Behind," he yelled, knowing Pudge would get himself behind the net for a pass. Before Jake or the defenceman got too close he gave the puck back to Pudge. The defenceman broke off and returned to the front of the net. Charlie had no doubt Jake would finish his check. In fact, he counted on it.

Jake's eyes were blazing as he left his feet to deliver the crushing check. Charlie stood still at first, then at the last second did a 360-degree spin. Jake brushed past his shoulder and smashed into the boards with such force Charlie heard him gasp for breath. He could not stay to enjoy that beautiful sound, however. There was a goal to score. Robert had moved further in, a metre past the top of the circle, which drew Liam away from the slot. Matt occupied the defenceman in front, so with

Jake out of the play Charlie was able to slip into open space in front.

Pudge anticipated his move perfectly and slid it over from the back wall. He had to take it on his backhand, unfortunately. There was no time to transfer to his forehand. He could sense the pressure. Pudge stormed back in front. Charlie took a half step to the right and drove to the inside post. The goalie dropped to the ice. He saw the smallest of openings between the goalie's right skate and the post. A flick of his stick sent the puck flying. The crowd roared, and Charlie began to lift his stick.

A huge groan from the Rebels supporters told Charlie all he needed to know. The puck had nicked the goalie's left toe and dribbled wide. Charlie could not believe the save. The puck should have been in. The Wildcats right defenceman raced behind the net to snag the rebound. Angry at himself for missing such a glorious chance, Charlie slid across to his left to cut off the passing lane up the middle, and then turned sideways, facing the boards, figuring the defenceman would pass to Jake on the flank, and Charlie would have the chance for a little payback. Without warning, the defenceman spun and swung at the puck.

Whack.

The puck bounced off the inside of Charlie's right skate and back to the defenceman, who this time passed it to Jake. The pain in Charlie's foot almost made him sick, and it took all his willpower not to drop to the ice. Jake wasted no time headmanning the puck to Roscoe. The turnover had been unexpected and sudden, and with Robert caught deep with Pudge and Matt, Liam and Roscoe had a two-on-one against Christopher.

Jake took off like a rocket. If he caught up it would be a three-on-one disaster. Charlie gritted his teeth and began to skate. He could barely put pressure on his right foot, and the only way he could move was to limp and push off his left as hard as he could. He heard some laughing in the stands; and he could only imagine how ridiculous he looked, bobbing up and down like a piston, pumping his arms, hobbling after Jake.

Liam took a feed from Roscoe and swung out to the left. Christopher remained in the middle of the two attackers, holding his stick in front of him, left arm held out to the side. Roscoe was really motoring down the right side, and Liam feathered a pass a couple of metres from the blue line. Christopher had to pivot to cut him off, and when he did, Roscoe flipped a forehand under his stick back to Liam. Christopher let him go and he spun back to stop Liam.

Liam slowed down, which allowed Christopher to get between him and Martin. That did not give Charlie any comfort. Jake had crossed the blue line. Charlie could see it clearly from his vantage point. Liam was setting Christopher up by getting him to commit, and then he would give it to Jake for a breakaway, with Roscoe camped out on the right hand side for a tap in.

"Use me," Jake yelled.

Martin had to stay with Liam or he could blast it into the short side. A pass to Jake and the puck was in the net. Liam curled the tip of his blade around the puck, drawing it toward his feet and freezing Christopher with a stutter-step. Then, without so much as a glance, he calmly slid the puck into the high slot. If

Charlie had not despised Liam, he might have admired that piece of skill. Moreover, he was still a good two metres behind Jake. He lowered his head and forced himself to skate normally. It was excruciating and Charlie felt lightheaded, but he had to stop that shot.

Christopher and his brother had proven their toughness countless times before. This time even Charlie could not believe it when Christopher dove forward, stick extended over his head, into the slot to try to stop Jake's shot. Jake held back, deciding instead to stick-handle around him to the left, which meant he had to transfer the puck to his backhand. For the first time Charlie felt he had a chance. Jake's move let him close the gap, and as a left-hander Charlie could use his forehand.

Jake was almost around Christopher. Charlie launched himself with a push off his left foot. "Next time," he gasped.

In one motion, he lifted Jake's stick, took a half stride and swept the puck with a backhand to the boards. Jake stood up straight, looking around for the puck, obviously in shock that someone had caught him. He also forgot about Christopher, who slid into him and took his feet out from under him. He went flying over Christopher and into Liam, and the two Wildcats forwards went down in a jumble of arms and legs.

The puck barely kissed the side wall and bounced back a few inches at the hash marks. Charlie curled tightly around the face-off dot and scooped it on his backhand. His foot was throbbing. It had been a long shift, and he was winded from the backcheck. On the other hand, all three Wildcats forwards were caught, and Pudge and Matt were waving their sticks in the neutral zone, with Robert hustling back.

Charlie fired it up ice to Pudge near the red line and then began his crazy bobbing to try to catch up. Pudge took it to the right side, faked an outside move, and when the defenceman did not bite, continued to the outside. The defenceman dropped low, hoping to crush Pudge against the boards with a hip check. Pudge did not even try to avoid the contact. He threw himself against the defender, keeping his feet moving the entire time. The contact sent Pudge banging against the boards but he stayed up and held the puck with an outstretched stick. To his credit the defenceman also kept his feet and, after regaining his stride, pivoted and extended his stick to stop Pudge from getting the angle and cutting in on goal.

Pudge then put on the brakes and banked it off the wall backward with a forehand to Matt, who came swooping in behind about two metres inside the top of the circle. He carved on his inside edges and headed for the net, with only the left defenceman to beat.

Charlie's legs were burning and his lungs were on fire. His foot felt like a solid object, like a big rock but with pins and needles sticking into it. He began to doubt his decision not to shift. Another turnover and he would never be able to get back. Just as he was about to break off to the bench, Matt slid the puck back to his feet, headfaked an outside move, and lobbed it into the high slot, as Liam had done before.

Charlie did not even feel the puck on his stick. He could not hear the crowd. He could barely think. His first instinct was to shoot, and as if by magic the goalie moved back in his goal, almost daring him to. Charlie brought the puck to his backhand, then to his forehand again. The goalie was not buying any of it and Charlie saw him move his blocker higher up the shaft. He'd go for a poke check, Charlie knew it.

Two metres from the crease Charlie threw on the brakes, showering the goalie with snow. The goalie dropped to his knees and extended his stick. At the same time Charlie spun with his back to the goalie, keeping the puck on his backhand and then extending his arms as far as he could to shovel the puck toward the corner of the glove side.

The Wildcats defenceman lowered the boom and knocked him clear off his feet. He landed with a thud, and slid on his back into the net. With his last particle of strength he raised his head. Pudge and Matt had their sticks over their heads and they were hugging each other. The goalie's head was bent, his weight supported his blocker and glove. Charlie lay back and closed his eyes. His heart was pounding so hard he could hear it. His body hurt from head to toe.

He felt awesome.

25

HOME

Charlie slouched against the dressing room wall and plopped his feet on his hockey bag.

"I insist on another side-five, three times over, with a two-snap finish," Scott said to him.

"Can't I relax?" Charlie complained.

"No," Scott said.

They slapped hands, pulling back sharply with two snaps to end it.

"That's the tenth time," Nick said. "Guys, I know I've said it before, but this time I'm serious. We have to kill Scott. It's the only way to stop it."

Scott gaped at him. "Dude, we crush the Wildcats 2–0 in the most epic game I've ever seen. I sweat through my shirt by the end of the first period. Charlie's last game and he sets up the first and scores the insurance goal, and now I need another side-five or I'm gonna burst into tears."

"Quick. Do it, Charlie," Nick pleaded. "He's so ugly when he cries."

"It is a nice feeling, though," Charlie said. "I wanted that game so bad my chest hurt."

"I lost two kilos just watching," Zachary said.

The last period had been played so close to the edge Charlie wondered how it ended the way it did. All the boys took it to the limit, every shift a contest of wills, a question of who wanted the puck more, who could fight through the fatigue, who could ignore the pain. Even Charlie had wanted to quit a hundred times. Only something deep inside spurred him on; not the fear of losing to Jake and the Wildcats, but rather the desire to prove his loyalty to the Rebels. Time after time he would come out of the corner with the puck, nicked up a bit more and his foot still throbbing; but the puck would get out of the Rebels end, and that made everything worth it.

"I really love the scent of your hockey bags," Zachary said, "but we have to leave at some point. The parents are probably getting a bit grouchy."

A lot of the guys had left, but a few had stayed behind, as if by some secret, unspoken arrangement. It was clear these guys wanted the moment to last a little longer. Charlie could have stayed in the dressing room all night, hanging out and trading stories. Sure, it was the last game he would play for the Rebels. But tonight was not going to be about feeling sorry for Charlie Joyce. It was going to be a celebration of what they had done together. He had a great idea.

"Listen, guys. I've got something on my mind that I really need to talk to you about . . ." he said in a hushed tone that quieted the group.

They all looked at him, grim-faced.

"What's up?" Zachary said apprehensively.

Charlie hesitated for a moment, and then put on as pathetic a voice as he could manage. "I was thinking that maybe we could go to the Mercury tonight. I just don't know whether to have a pizza or take it meaty and go for the burger."

There was a collective sigh of relief.

"Joyce, that's thinking small," Scott said. "Order both and have no regrets."

"Obviously," Spencer said.

"It's the only answer," Brandon added.

"Yeah, Joyce, use your brain," Matt said.

"I'm ashamed," Charlie said.

"I'm ashamed of you, too," Scott said.

"Why don't we ask our parents and then be ashamed while we walk," Nick said. "I'm getting hungry."

Charlie was relieved, happy that his little joke had worked, and the boys got up to leave. But Julia beat them to the door, coming in with Rebecca and Alexandra in tow.

"Your parents are wondering if you're ever going to come out. They sent us in to investigate," Julia said.

"We got to talking," Charlie said. "We were about to go."

"Whenever we discuss politics the time tends to get away from us. That was an excellent point about the election, Nicholas," Scott said.

"Thank you, Mr. Slatsky," Nick said, "and well done on that PowerPoint presentation, Zachary. I'll never think of the Roman Empire the same way."

"Are we being mocked?" Julia asked the other two girls.

"It appears so," Rebecca answered. "Very shocking under the circumstances."

"Maybe we should reconsider," Alexandra said.

"I'm tempted," Julia said, "but I feel sorry for them. It must be hard having to go through life so stupid."

"If you have to, okay. I say it's a huge mistake," Alexandra said.

"Rebecca's uncle is sponsoring a showing of *A Christmas Carol* at the Grand tonight," Julia said. "He just called and will give us a bunch of tickets, whatever we want. We wondered if some of the Rebels might want to come since there's no school tomorrow . . .?"

A few of the guys shot Charlie a look. He shook his head ever so slightly. He did not want to tell the girls, at least not Julia, not like this. He would call her tomorrow. And as for the movie, to be honest he would rather hang with his buds, talking hockey and the Rebels. But Julia might take it the wrong way; and it was nice of Rebecca's uncle; and Alexandra probably wanted to talk with Brandon . . . Why was it never straightforward?

"We were going to get something to eat . . . We were hungry after the game . . . not sure if there's time for that and a movie?" he said.

"No problem," Julia said cheerfully. "The movie's not till 9:30. If we leave now we can get a bite and still make it."

She seemed so stoked about it, and the girls had worked so hard at the café. He did not have the heart. "Sounds great," Charlie said. "Might cost us dessert, but it's the holidays."

Scott's shoulders sagged. "No dessert? This is a nightmare."

"There's free popcorn at the theatre," Rebecca said.

"Are you an angel?" Scott said.

"It's about time you realized that," Julia said. Her eyes sparkled. "We'll meet you gentlemen in the lobby. Hurry up."

The boys grabbed their bags and filed out.

Pudge hung back, and Charlie did the same, guessing his buddy wanted to say something.

"Nice win," Charlie said.

"I'll remember it for a while — maybe forever."

Charlie looked down at the floor. "I might be moving to Stanville, but it won't really change anything, not with us. Right?"

He looked back up at his friend. Pudge's eyes were glistening. "No chance, Captain."

"So let's go get some grub, Sergeant," he said. He held out his fist, and Pudge gave it a punch.

Charlie went out first. He didn't want the other guys to notice anything about Pudge, so to distract them he began to sniff the air. "Do you smell that?"

"Scott!" Nick said.

"Not this time, I swear," Scott said.

Charlie kept sniffing. "I can't believe you guys don't smell it. I've never smelled it so strong before."

Zachary sniffed the air. "All I get is arena."

"I don't smell anything either," Pudge said.

Charlie shrugged. "That's the odour of barbecued Wildcats."

"And there's no sweeter smell than that," Scott said. "Now guess who needs another side-five with a double snap finish?"

* * *

A gust of wind hit Charlie in the face as he and Pudge turned the corner. On top of it all it had begun to snow.

The flakes flew into his eyes, making it painful to keep them open, so much so that he had to turn around and walk backward.

"What happened? Temperature's dropped like a million degrees since I came to the rink," Pudge said.

"We should abandon ship," Scott said. "Conditions are too extreme, and I think Nick's crying for his mommy."

"Just great. My brain is frozen and I can't think of a comeback," Nick said.

"You guys really are babies," Julia said. "Fresh air is good for you."

"You said you had a way better place than the Mercury," Spencer said. "You didn't say it was at the North Pole."

"Buck up, young man," Alexandra said. "It's around the corner."

Around the corner they went. The street was deserted apart from a couple of cars parked on the side and a few people scurrying a block away, their hoods pulled tightly over their heads.

"Is it bad when you can't feel your feet?" Matt said.

"I wish I still had feet," Scott said. "Mine snapped off about three blocks ago."

"I promise it will be worth it," Julia said.

"Where are we going?" Charlie said. They were on the same street as the Rainbow Café. He knew every restaurant and fast food spot around here.

"It's new, and we're going to be practically the first customers," Julia said.

"Then how do you know it's so awesome?" Brandon said.

Julia ignored him and the girls pressed on. As they got closer to the Rainbow Café, the boys stopped talking. Charlie knew they were feeling awkward about not being able to fix it. It was not their fault and they knew that too, but that's what his buds were like.

If only he had not lost his temper at Jake that night; if only he had not left the stove on. The *if only*s were enough to make him lose his mind.

Oddly, the girls were oblivious to it all. Even the normally quiet Rebecca was chatting away and joking with Alexandra and Julia. Come to think of it, Julia was acting downright weird, giggling at anything and talking about totally random stuff, like her science teacher looking like Kermit the Frog, or the snow being so fluffy it looked like floating tissue paper. Charlie was freezing, and so were his teammates, and yet the girls did not seem to feel the cold at all. Very weird. He was about to mention it when Julia clapped and pointed at a building up ahead.

"There it is," she said. "You'll love it. I swear. Best place ever."

Charlie didn't see anything, and he knew this block like the back of his hand. Suddenly, the girls took off and ran.

"Did three girls who used to be fairly normal just become insane maniacs?" Charlie said.

"Girl behaviour is never easy to understand, but they've definitely lost their minds tonight," Spencer said.

"It's official, dudes. I've frozen to death," Zachary said.

Charlie saw the girls stop in front of the Rainbow

Café. Then it hit him. His heart sank. They already knew. Maybe Brandon had texted Alexandra, or one of the other guys told them at the rink, or maybe Pudge had told his dad who then told other parents. This was going to be too painful for words.

"So . . . what's the deal, ladies?" he called out.

"Come here and stop talking so much," Julia answered.

She was acting beyond weird.

All he wanted was to be with his friends and have a few laughs and to forget about things, just for one night. He forced himself to be quiet. One word and his irritation would come out.

"Charlie, I got to thinking after we stopped working," Julia began.

"It's cold," Charlie said.

"Hush," Julia said. "Anyway, Spencer said the problem was we didn't have the skills. We had the effort, but not the talent. So I asked myself, what if we got some talent and then combined it with our effort?"

"What an interesting thought," Alexandra said.

"I thought so," Julia said.

The snow was picking up, and the girls' hats were covered in white. Charlie could only look on enviously. He had left his hat at home, as usual.

"So I paid a visit to the guy who was working at the car dealership, where the new Dunn's Sportsmart is going in, and asked him if he knew of any talent and . . . Ta-da!" With a huge smile she opened the door and, holding it with her foot, spread her arms wide.

The boys did not move. Charlie stepped forward. "Julia?" he began.

She leaned forward. "Ta-da was your cue to go in, dummy."

He was almost scared as he walked past her and opened the inner door.

Bright lights flicked on, nearly blinding him, and he had to blink a few times to focus. The café was filled with men. Off to the side were the rest of the Rebels and Hilton and Jeffrey, and in front of the window, Matt's dad, and next to him, his mom and Danielle.

"Yo, Charlie. Close your mouth, you're catching flies," Danielle said.

Everyone began to laugh. His friends had all come in by now.

"Any of you guys have a clue what's going on?" he said to them.

"We must have died from the cold on the walk over and this is heaven," Scott said.

"I thought heaven would have a few more puffy clouds, and the angels would be . . . better looking," Nick said.

"I think my heart skipped about ten beats when I walked in," his mom said. "Matt's dad called to tell me some of his tools were left behind and he really needed them. I came over to pick them up . . ."

"I figured it out," Danielle bragged.

"But . . . what . . . the movie?" Charlie sputtered.

"Okay, Charlie: there's no movie," Julia said. "Never was. Never will be. Rent it. Buy it. Move on. We're here to fix the Rainbow Café once and for all. You can go to the Grand later."

He stared at his mom. "Did the insurance . . .?"

"No dear. They had nothing to do with it. It's your

wonderful friends who organized things — and Paulo."

A man held out his hand. Charlie recognized him as the contractor from the car dealership. They shook.

"I'm Paulo. I understand you and your buddies are here to help. We could use your help if we're going to get this done by tomorrow morning."

"How is this even possible?" Charlie asked.

"This young lady came by yesterday and asked if we could help out." He pointed to Julia. "I spoke to the guys, and they were all in favour; and then we got lucky 'cause the new windows didn't arrive today, so we don't have to work tomorrow. Anyway, we figured it was a good cause and a way to give back to the community. We can't deprive the good people of Terrence Falls of their coffee and treats, and Burt here tells me your mom makes the best cupcakes in town. I'm a sucker for red velvet with cream cheese frosting."

A burly, broad-shouldered man held up a hammer. Burt certainly looked like he enjoyed his pastries.

Charlie took a moment to collect himself. The men had already started their work. He could see that most of the damaged ceiling tiles had been replaced. Three table saws lined one side of the dining area. Near the window, they had stacked the used pieces of lumber, and by the kitchen was a neat and tidy stack of perfectly clean lumber with all the nails removed. Judging from all the wood shavings and sawdust on the floor, they had used the table saws to cut the lumber down to size so they could use it properly.

"What do you want us to do?" Charlie asked Paulo finally.

"This is a hockey team, right?" Paulo said. "Give me

one line to help with the ceiling, another on that wall to help with drywall repair and a third to deal with the floor. Defencemen can come with me for general maintenance." He grinned. "I might've been a rushing defenceman back in the day, by the way."

"We're with ya, dude," Scott said, and he and Nick saluted.

"Are you really both defencemen?" Paulo said.

"I know how annoying Nick can be," Scott said. "Just tell him to shut up. It won't work, though. He simply will not be quiet . . ."

"Give me strength," Paulo said, eyes raised to the ceiling. "Okay. Coaches, you're with Stanislaw to help with the carpentry." Matt's dad waved his hand. "And ladies, this here is Jude. He's gonna fix the appliances and clean up."

"Now listen up, people," Scott said. "I'll be second in command, so pay extra attention to me. I'll try to keep things simple because you're mostly too thick to understand me, especially Nick."

"I've got an idea," Paulo said, wrapping an arm around Scott's shoulders and leading him to the kitchen. "How do you feel about really dirty, messy, difficult jobs?"

"That's more Nick's specialty," Scott whimpered.

Charlie, Pudge, Zachary and Jonathon were assigned to the flooring team. A man wearing kneepads was on the floor banging a chisel with a big thick mallet. With each blow a piece of tile flew into the air, and in practically no time the rest of the broken tile was cleared away. The man then brushed some glue into the space.

"Wait five minutes and then put the new tile in," he said gruffly. "Make sure it's in the centre." He got up and began chiselling out another damaged tile.

"Did any of you guys know about this?" Charlie said.

"Not me," Pudge said, still wearing the same stunned expression he had when he walked in to the café. Zachary and Jonathon both shook their heads.

Charlie wondered if he looked as bewildered as Pudge. He felt it. This was all so unbelievable.

"Good call, Paulo," Charlie heard Scott say. "That's exactly what I would have done if I'd known what to do."

"Are you going to be here all night?" Paulo replied.

"You'd have to put a bullet in my head to get me outta here," Scott said.

"Paulo, don't dismiss the idea right away. Consider the advantages," Nick said.

Paulo's booming laughter seemed to energize the crew, and they kept up a hectic pace for the next hour. Most of the broken floor tiles were fixed in short order, and each new one fit perfectly. Charlie had just plopped in another when he felt a light tap on his shoulder. A tall woman with round glasses and a toothy smile waved at him.

"You're the reporter from the *Examiner*. Lorie, right?" he said.

"Guilty as charged."

"I . . . um . . . didn't expect you . . . Are you here to help too? It's awful nice of you. I don't really know what you can do. We have lots of people . . ."

She clapped her hands gleefully and laughed as if

Charlie had made the funniest joke ever. "I'd love to help, but I'd likely cause more damage. I'm here on official business. I want to cover the story: the community pulling together; a family fighting to stay in Terrence Falls, the town they've grown to love. The story writes itself."

"How'd you hear about it?" he said.

She looked at her notebook. "A certain Julia Chow called the paper tonight. This story will be huge. Everyone will be talking about it, and I predict lineups around the block when the Rainbow Café opens. Trust me. This'll be a gold mine. Anyway, your mom said I could take a few pictures and talk to you guys for some quotes. Can you crowd together for a pic?"

They stood together, arm in arm. Charlie felt silly, and he knew he was grinning like a fiend.

"Thanks, Lorie," he said, and she flashed a thumbs-up and went off to photograph Spencer's team as they put in another piece of drywall.

Charlie's group had one tile to go. As the man chiselled it out, Charlie noticed Julia sweeping up some broken ceiling tiles in the main room. He slipped out of the kitchen.

"Don't expect me to say thanks or anything just because this is the most amazing thing ever," Charlie said to Julia.

"As if I care where you live," Julia said.

"It's a nice Christmas present," he said. He had a feeling a few guys were watching, but he didn't care. "I guess I should give you something too," he said.

"Any ideas? I love presents."

"I was figuring on a pack of gum and a bag of chips."

She looked impressed. "That's very generous — and I'll take it . . . but maybe you could also take me to that party . . ."

"Maybe . . . I will."

Zachary popped his head out between the kitchen doors. "Hey, tile boy. You wanna put in the last one?"

"Get back to work," Julia said softly. She blushed and began sweeping again, and he went to the kitchen to finish the tiling.

But it sure did not feel like work. At this pace they would get it all done by morning. His mom would be able to reopen soon, she would make enough money to pay the bank, and he could barely stop himself from screaming at the top of his lungs.

Charlie Joyce wasn't going anywhere!

26

THE LOVE OF THE GAME

Brandon outhustled the Thunder centre for the puck and he backhanded it to Philip at the Rebels' blue line. Philip rifled it across the ice to Spencer, who took it on the fly and pressed forward along the right boards. A metre across the red line he dumped it in. The puck whizzed around the wall behind the net, and Nazem was able to get to it first.

"We've got Matt and Pudge next up as wingers, with Charlie at centre," Hilton announced, pacing as usual behind his players.

"We need to open it up," Charlie said to his line-mates. "Let's try to carry it in and attack down low, with the trailer getting in front. They aren't the fastest, so keep an eye open for the counterattack."

The Thunder right defenceman did a good job against Nazem and he was able to shovel the puck behind the net to his partner. He gave his centre a sharp pass at the hash marks. Brandon gave chase, and he caught him just over the Thunder's blue line. The puck carrier fought hard and was able to get to centre, but then, either ready to change or simply tired of Brandon's backchecking, he dumped the puck in between

Spencer and Philip and peeled off to the bench. His linemates did the same. Brandon was winded too and he headed over.

"Heads up, Charlie," Hilton's voice rang out.

Charlie was over the boards before his words were out.

"Good shift," Charlie told Brandon as he sped by.

He heard a cowbell from the stands. Spencer caught up with the puck about three metres in front of the crease. He took it on his forehand and swung wide right. Charlie noticed Philip cheating up on the left. He must want a change, and Charlie figured Spencer was bagged too. Charlie charged inside the blue line, spun backward and waved his stick. Spencer obliged with a pass and immediately took off for the bench.

Charlie continued skating backward with the puck. He was in no real hurry because he needed to give the twins time to get on, and he was also wary of being last man. The Thunder centre came forward to pressure him. Robert raced to the right corner. Charlie waited until the forechecker committed and passed it to Robert. Pudge then set up on the left, with Matt on the right. Charlie glided into the slot.

The Thunder left winger cruised in to join the forecheck, forcing Robert to pass to his brother behind the net. The winger backed off and the centre stood in front, waiting for Christopher to make his move. A light went off in Charlie's head, as if he was seeing a movie. This was Pressure 2, the breakout Hilton had been trying to teach them. Christopher faked a half step to his left and came around the net to Andrew's right. Charlie had to make a quick decision. The play called for him to criss-cross with Pudge. But then he'd leave the slot uncovered. On the other hand, Hilton had been preaching for them to trust each other.

Charlie had to swerve not to run into Pudge. His bud had also committed to the play. Charlie cut up the right side in time to see Christopher drop pass to Robert when the centre forechecked him. Robert promptly carved sharply to his left and snapped a pass to Pudge about two metres inside the Rebels' zone. Matt had cruised into the neutral zone and Pudge gave it to him. He wasted no time, one-timing a pass to Charlie at centre. Fooled by the quick puck movement, the Thunder right winger had let him go, and the left defenceman was backing off, so Charlie had lots of room. He kept outside, picking up the pace, making as if he was going it alone. He gained the blue line, and then at the hash marks slammed on the brakes. Matt slowed slightly.

"To the net," he yelled, and Matt took off like a shot.

That cleared the way for Pudge as the trailer, just like they had talked about. He gave it to him once Pudge had crossed the line and then cut behind the left defenceman, who had a tough choice. Pudge was barrelling toward the net with the puck, but he also had to worry about Charlie sneaking behind him. He opted to deal with Pudge and charged out, going down on one knee, his glove to his side, his stick blocking the passing lane.

The ice sprayed a metre high as Pudge stopped short and saucered the puck over the defenceman's stick. Charlie took it and continued on net without breaking stride. The other defenceman in front with

Matt pivoted on his right foot. Charlie saw that he was going to throw himself on the ice to block a pass across. The goalie was already well out of the net playing shot all the way. Charlie didn't hesitate. Before the defence-man could sprawl, Charlie slid the puck under his shin pads. Matt had turned sideways, facing Charlie. In perfect position, he had time to stop the puck, take aim and, with a snap of the wrist, roof it under the crossbar.

Matt had missed almost two months with a concussion, and this was his first goal since his return. Charlie could not contain his joy. He leapt in the air and pumped his fist.

"Welcome back," he screamed and gave Matt a bear hug.

"If I knew you could pass I'd have come back sooner," Matt joked.

Pudge draped his arms across their shoulders. "Are you still playing with the Rebels?" he said to Charlie.

"I'll stick around until I get a better offer."

They all laughed and skated to the blue line where Christopher and Robert congratulated them.

"That was fun to watch," Robert said.

His brother tapped their shin pads, which was about as expressive as he ever got, but his eyes were shining. Charlie drifted slowly back to centre. This was one moment he wanted to savour. A couple weeks ago he was leaving Terrence Falls. Then Paulo and his boys had pulled it off with a marathon work night and fixed the café. The Rainbow reopened to huge crowds. Lorie's story had been front-page news, and it was as if the entire town had rediscovered his mom's place all at once. Since then his mom had made enough money to catch up on her bank payments — she had even been able to buy Christmas presents.

"Go, Rebels, go! Go, Rebels, go! Go, Rebels, go!"

Scott and Nick were conducting the cheering crowd. Rebecca pulled Scott's hat over his eyes, and he spun and began to conduct with his back to them all. Julia and Alexandra kept the cheer going while Danielle kept the beat with her cowbell. The referee's whistle startled him. Charlie could have kicked himself. It was the middle of a game, and he was watching the crowd.

"Set up, number eight," the ref said.

There was nothing he would rather do. It was 1–0 in the second period, playing with the Rebels, for his favourite coach, and with his mom and sister — and Julia — watching. The referee held the puck over the dot. Charlie had his stick in a reverse grip. On a whim he straightened up, backed up a touch and, holding the stick normally, went with the forehand sweep. Caught by surprise, the other centre could not match his quickness, and the puck whirled straight to Robert. The left winger pressured. Robert banked a pass off the wall to Matt. The right defenceman moved up, but Matt brought the bouncing puck under control in time and batted it deep before absorbing the hit.

Charlie raced after it. He felt like he could fly, as if his skates had rockets in the blades.

ABOUT THE AUTHOR

David Skuy spent most of his childhood playing one sport or another — hockey, soccer, football, rugby. Now he is a writer and lawyer who lives in Toronto, Ontario with his wife and two kids. He still plays hockey once a week and remains a die-hard Leafs fan.

He began writing the Game Time series to try to capture the competition, the challenges, the friendships and the rivalries that make sports so much fun.

His book *Undergrounders* won the Silver Birch Award in 2012.

The Game Time series:

Off the Crossbar
Rebel Power Play
Making the Cut
Overtime